YESTERDAY, 72 YEARS AGO

ERIK WHITMAN

For all the persecuted nations throughout history: Jews, Africans, Native Americans, Middle Eastern peoples, and - last but not least - the Roma. May peace reign in this cold, cold world once and for all.

If there's a book that you want to read, but it hasn't been written yet, then you must write it.

— TONI MORRISON

CHAPTER 1

"Such is the way of creation: First comes darkness, then light." - Talmud Shabbat 77b

Aging is a long party of funerals and goodbyes. My grandmother Hannah Goldmann passed away in her home on Rossmore Avenue, in the Hancock Park neighborhood of Los Angeles. Today I came to her place for the first time in 20 years. She had been a recluse for most of her final days and we hadn't seen each other for about the same period. As I opened the cast iron main gate, I noticed the mirrors inside the house were left covered since her funeral last week.

The 1924 Queen Anne mansion sat on a 20,000-square-foot lot with an olympic pool, a spa, and a guesthouse for 4 people. My favorite meditative spot in the property used to be the lush red rose garden, which was embraced by high, majestic sycamores - nothing shy of Heaven to me. With a slight heaviness in my chest, I gently pushed the main entry door carved in ebony wood in a sinuous leaf design, reminiscent of days old - a charm not often found in homes nowadays! There were 8 bedrooms with their respective fireplaces; 5 bathrooms, all but one with a bathtub adorned with copper fixtures; a breakfast nook; and dark wood-paneled walls. Majestic, stately, an exquisite home!

Hannah had a magnetic presence. She demanded that you looked at her, not as an authoritative figure but as someone whose wisdom surpassed her years on this cold Earth. I always thought of her smile when looking carefully at the pictures of those enlightened by the light of God, of those who did a mitzvah to anyone no matter who, of those who made humanitarianism their mission. The aroma of gardenias and fresh coffee still lingered in the air. Following my gut feeling, I went upstairs. Much to my dismay, I took a look at the walls only to find out the wallpaper was peeling off and the light fixtures smelled like mold, something inconceivable for those who knew Hannah's pride in keeping things neat, "as close to God as possible!" It was really sad to see the walls in that state. Had I known her health was deteriorating I would have made the first step to reconnect with her. Her isolation in her late years made no sense to me. It's still a mystery why someone so active would confine herself to one room in such a huge property. The image I have of her is that of a sage with a girly smile that captivated everyone. Her wide eyes warmed everyone's heart. Her shy smile was disarming.

I remember when she took me to Malibu on Yom Kippur one day and said, "Look at the ocean, Michael. It'll always be there for you whenever you need it. And the waves are inconsistent yet perfect in their imperfection. Like them, we thrive for improvement each day. Because perfection is an illusion." I never forgot her remark. Then we cast off our sins from the previous year by throwing bread crumbs into the flowing waters of the Pacific Ocean. It was 1978, I was only

10 years old. When I think of it, what sort of sins could someone my age then possess? Through the years, I came to believe she was teaching me a lesson. People often play games of perfection then drown themselves and others in their insecurities. Because perfection is unattainable.

Today I came to take possession of her house, as her sole descendant. The place resembled a ghost ship without her. I caressed the walls with my fingertips and the disgusting glue from the wallpaper stuck to my hand. I rushed to one of the bathrooms to rinse off my hands. The smell of mildew was unbearable, coming from the ceiling and infesting the room with sadness. Even the soap was rancid. I turned the faucet on, waited a second to allow the water to become clean. From 2003 on, the year when I left to live in London, no one had set foot on the upper floors. The whole place had a strong foundation though, and I think it would take only a few repairs to return it to its living glory. A sparrow came in through a crack on the window, with a hurt wing.

"Hey, little friend. Come here. Ohhh…"

I managed to capture the little creature in the palm of my hands. I felt his tiny heart trembling in captivity, fighting for freedom.

"Hush, hush. I mean no harm."

Suddenly I thought of the bird cage I had when I was 10 years old, which I used to keep in a corner in the kitchen downstairs. Three doors to the left side of the hall upstairs was the location of the room I once called my own. Strangely, it stood the test of time. The furniture, the bed sheets, my bookcase with all of my favorite authors, even the reclining chair that was my grandfather's, everything was intact. Albeit the light coming from the window was different this time. It didn't have the same magic as before, as though it had lost its luster.

I headed downstairs holding the sparrow in my big manly

hands as gently as I could. Under the breakfast nook table I found the mint green metal birdcage. I placed my new friend inside it with paternal care. He chirped. I smiled. The house had many memories and, as frequently happens to such places after the owner dies, it left a rich psychological imprint on everyone who had ventured into its secretive chambers. At the breakfast nook table, I had the first latkes I ever made by myself. The smell was still lingering in my mind to this day. The first aid kit was in the same drawer below, the one containing grandma's daily pills. And I recalled the afternoon when she slipped in the kitchen while making matzo ball soup for our Seder and I darted to the drawer to grab the kit to care for her bruises.

I once read that sparrows have a spiritual meaning, that they represent balance in one's personal life, career, and relationships, that they are also seen as omens of good luck, peace, and ease. Some believe sparrows carry away the souls of the dead. If so, I hope my new friend here whom I nicknamed Mr. Chirps will carry away Hannah's soul to an enlightened place. I caught a glimpse of his reddish back feathers, which confirmed my assumption about his gender.

"Yes, I was right! You are a boy, Mr. Chirps!"

His left wing looked broken. As I was about to immobilize it, he then proved me wrong and flew all over the kitchen chirping and singing his melody. I stood there just contemplating the sweet song he produced and closed my eyes in bliss. For a moment, I wasn't Michael anymore, I became the bird - free, unafraid, without any worldly agenda, no games, nothing. When his tune subsided, I opened my eyes only to find out he had flown above the main staircase so I ran upstairs as fast as I could. Chirps had reached the attic. I followed him up there. There was an aura of mystery about that space. Next, Chirps landed on an old rocking chair near a decaying crib. Except for those two pieces of furniture, there were several cardboard boxes with names on them. One of the boxes read "Sadie," in black highlight pen. Inside it, a scratched mahogany music box with a miniature key resting in the keyhole. An oval mirror, a pedestal with a porcelain-like ballerina, and handmade wicker cot with a figurine that resembled a baby. For some awkward reason, I had a feeling of restlessness as I turned on the music: an eerie version of Rock-a-Bye Baby sent me shivers down the spine. Grandma Hannah once told me one of the theories about the origins of this nursery rhyme lies on the fact that Native Americans used to rock their babies in birch-bark cradles up the branches of a tree, and that it was adopted by the Mayflower colonists.

Sadie's box also contained a baby's comb in light pink, and what caught my attention right away was a book similar to a diary. It had dehydrated leaves for cover. The paper inside was rough, almost suitable for watercolor paintings. There were stains of rust and time in it. I then decided to open its pages and read,

"1918. The beginning of it all."

All of a sudden, a cold draft blew in through the crack of the red glass window, announcing the imminent storm with a vengeance. The rest of the window glass shattered completely, letting the wind in so unexpectedly that Mr. Chirps flew back downstairs without uttering a song. I wrapped myself in a frayed woman's shawl, grab the diary and fled the scene.

It rained the whole night. A torrential storm of sorts, uncommon in Southern California. The turbulent flowing streams washed the gloom in the air, and I could forecast how clear the skies would be much later. I thought to myself, "Who was Sadie? How come I never heard of her? '1918. The beginning of it all?' Beginning of what?"

I fell asleep on the living room couch as the rain cleansed

my memories of London, my wife, two children, and my demanding job as a marketing company Exec. It was an unsettling sleep. I kept seeing grandma at my Bar Mitzvah party but instead of me on the chair up high, she was the one on it. And she gave me a disturbing grin, bordering psychotic. Then strips of silvery metallic wrapping paper with blue stars of David, a symbol of martyrdom and heroism, floated around her like a blessing. I remained stagnant for an uncomfortable long time, as she paraded on during my Bar Mitzvah up on the chair. I woke up startled. My tears rolled down my face and landed on my lap very determined about their suicide leap, as if off the cliff of my cheekbones down to the rocks below nearing the dark blue Pacific Ocean. I snatched my handkerchief from my pants' pocket to wipe off my misery. I poured my sorrow into a glass of whiskey then drifted away, my thoughts blending in with the fog of confusion.

At dawn, the rain had dissipated. I dragged my exhausted self to the kitchen. The robust aroma of freshly brewed coffee, the sun rays penetrating the clouds, the glistening leaves on the trees outside, everything was an invitation to be hopeful. My cell rang. I made all the efforts to get the approval from London to remain in Los Angeles "in order to finalize the will," the only excuse I came up with. I served myself a cup of Joe, stirred in three spoons of regular sugar and my mind was clear again. A light headache was the only competition to my tranquil state of mind so I took a headache pill and went back to sleep.

This time, my fatigue proved a solid antidote against insomnia. I slept a true restorative slumber, just like a baby. Still, my fixation with the mysterious Sadie and her diary persisted as a haunting memory that revisited me in my sleep. I remember dreaming of the diary irradiating the sunlight that hit it straight from the sky. Its pages then came undone with the intensity of the golden light. I experienced a sense of relief as if that same golden light had filled me with Life itself, removing all that was bad to make room for the good and new. Often times we allow external forces to destroy our inner peace, however that's exactly when we must fight back to remove any obstacles to our peace of mind. Evil likes to disrupt calmness, and who is the best candidate than those who seek peace and harmony? I was always similar to grandma when it comes to the way I analyzed the world around me. My facial expressions used to die as I plunged deeper and deeper into others' psyche. That allowed me to take a lot in and understand people much better than they would understand themselves, and to them that was a bit invasive. When one meets an empath who instantly understands them in a deeper level, the former is seldom ready to confront their inner truth so they start hating the empath because the unconditional kindness serves as a mirror to how ugly people can be. That is a realization that may cause people to commit all sorts of crimes. For seeking the truth, you will certainly be persecuted, and that's a given! I am an empath much like grandma was. Having that in mind and despite her active humanitarianism, she avoided sharing her own experiences with anyone - family or other-wise - and rapidly changed the subject when she deemed appropriate. It was a self-preserving mechanism, I believe. But what could she be hiding, if anything? I assume the reader knows the expression "tears of a clown"? Behind that smiling face of hers hid a depth, a longing for something that never was, a chilling grief that could cut the air like a knife. But what would it be? Or am I overanalyzing it all? Some-times things get lost in the details, which may prevent us from seeing the big picture. I decided to take it at face value and accept her smile as a mere smile, nothing more.

I awoke to the sounds of Mr. Chirps. All in all, I couldn't

consider this a nightmare, for the outcome was positive; and the sleep, invigorating. The diary was in my hands, still intact. Its vanishing was only a dream. Minutes later, I was sipping my first coffee cup of the day. The caffeine activated my brain like an injection of Las Vegas on steroids. I couldn't stop thinking of all those boxes with names on them lying on the floor upstairs in the attic. There was still plenty of food in the fridge for me to fix myself a Reuben sandwich. The kosher kitchen was the only aspect of the house that didn't match Hannah's unorthodox ways. She observed the holidays and practices but that decision came from her deep sense of her Jewish identity and background rather than for a mere adherence to strict rules to fit in. She used to say that rules were restrictive, identical to the boa in "The Little Prince" which was, she knew it, my favorite book as a child. She encouraged everyone to be true to themselves then God would bestow upon them the sweetest of blessings. She attended the services on High Holy Days but didn't seem too attached to temples more than to its members and their charitable efforts. She was someone you could never buy. Neither with money, fame, luxury, nor with the promise of a friendship, or love. She beat to her own drum. I am much like her in that respect.

Mr. Chirps elected the unlocked birdcage to build his home. He tucked his bill underneath his scapular feathers then fell asleep inside the open cage.

I reopened the diary. One of the front pages was stuck to the next. I cautiously separated them both, only to realize the puzzle was getting more intriguing. I noticed the signature on the front page, "Sadie Goldmann." Goldmann? Strangely, I felt I wasn't prepared to read it yet. On the other hand, I was imbued with an adventurous whim to fumble its pages voraciously. Finally, I decided to set it on the dining table and went upstairs to check, out of curiosity, what else I could find in grandma's attic that didn't belong to Sadie. I wasn't ready for her yet.

I proceeded to unveil the next box, labeled "Avner." There were vintage photographs of my grandfather sitting at his desk working on his books. He looked fully committed to his craft, almost in an alternative dimension to where he escaped to return to his innermost self and find the peace, only known by those who toiled all their lives at a desk, those who didn't seem able to feel pain or any discomfort overworking. He used to type incessantly. I still remember the keys hammering on the black and red tape of his 1938 Underwood Champion. It was a muscular and solid typewriter, all in black, and the keys were easy for big-handed writers. I moved two of his autographed books out of the way. His typewriter was under them, which explained why the box was so hard to move. More photos, an old tape hanging from the side of the machine. A rolled canvas that depicted grandma Hannah with him gazing at each other in total bliss.

The following box was easier to figure out. It was labeled "Evie," after my mother. I decided not to open it because I still haven't dealt with her early passing. I was raised by grandma Hannah and grandpa Avi. Evie's box was surprisingly featherweight. I released a shy tear as I dealt with my feelings of losing my mother so abruptly. I fought against feeling robbed of her presence and the memories we never had the opportunity to experience together. The sun broke free from behind the clouds. The birds flew in through the window. A beam of light invaded the place and formed a spotlight on Evie's box.

For whatever reason, I wasn't ready to open Sadie's. I glanced at the last box. It read, "Shlomo and Ruth," my great grandparents. Inside it, old photographs of grandpa's jewelry business in the 4th *arrondissement* in Paris near the synagogue he attended while in the city for business. The synagogue was located on 10 Rue Pavée and was drafted in 1913 by architect Hector Guimard who designed many of Paris metro stations. As I went through the pictures, I noticed one of Shlomo, Hannah, and grandma Ruth standing behind her, gently touching her ears. Hannah was wearing a pair of shiny earrings, almost spectral in the fading photograph. A few keepsakes here and there, nothing of value, and a wooden dreidel she used to play with on Hanukkah, as she used to tell me. I also discovered his cotton tallit in mint condition and his stained rickety Cartier watch, a reminder that this beautiful timepiece had lost its significance.

We always attach value to objects in our lives and end up many times being objectified ourselves.

It was around noon when the clock downstairs rang solemnly. "Maybe it's about time…," I told myself as I opened Sadie's box. There were no photographs, no physical representation of her, which made it impossible for me to uncover her identity. Could it be that her truth was in her diary? It seemed to me that Sadie had vanished from the world, taking all of her belongings with her to the afterlife. Or could she still be alive? I ran downstairs to recover the diary. When I arrived at the dining table downstairs, Sadie's journal was staring at me just the way I left it, immobile like the air in the entire place. I sat down to read it.

As a note to the reader, I wrote this first chapter to explain how I came to find Sadie's diary. Please forgive me my rambling, my lack of structure. I am enjoying myself reminiscing. Hannah was a key figure in my life. The only thing I will always regret is not having her any longer with me, is having made the choice to move to London for a great job opportunity where I recreated myself down the whirlwind of daily routines and long working hours then got married, had two kids, and lost track of someone who was so dear to me like she was.

The following chapters were not written by me but are faithful reproductions of Sadie's diary, which I believe will change your world forever, as it did mine.

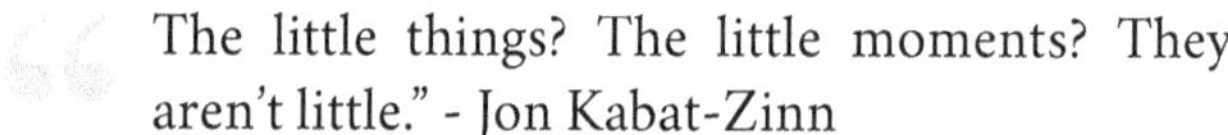
The little things? The little moments? They aren't little." - Jon Kabat-Zinn

On November 11, 1918, Britain, France, the US, and other allies defeated Germany. It was the end of the First World War, known as "the war to end all wars." Germany's loss represented a huge blow to its national pride. Thus, several future events catapulted the rise of the Third Reich. Its xenophobic sentiment fermented in the air, omnipresent in the Old World. To illustrate my point, in 1922 Benito Mussolini rose to power. Soon after, in 1926 Emperor Hirohito repeated the feat. In 1933, it was Adolf Hitler's turn.

I was born Sadie Goldmann on August 16, 1927, the second in line out of eight siblings. First came Ezra, followed by me then Elisabeth, Sarah, Amos, Ephraim, Rachel, Leah, and Abraham. My siblings and I differed from each other in the way we handled our perception of the Self and that of the world around us. Ezra was the first born, the golden boy in our family. He truly was the best brother I could ever have asked for: responsible, loving, caring, smart yet generous to a fault. Elizabeth, a year younger than I, enjoyed singing all day long. No one could ever make her stop, and she enchanted everyone around her with her lovely voice. In the face of any adversity, I believe Elizabeth would have laughed and kept humming her tune as if nothing were ever able to shake her inner peace. Sarah had meningitis at a young age, which severely damaged her hearing in the her right ear. Yet, somehow she was always the only one able to retell all the jokes and conversations she heard, word for word. And she was funny! She spoke with a girly, high-pitched voice that was bird-like but dissonant. When retelling a story, her voice sounded like Thelonius Monk hitting the keys with such force, so hard and boldly, as would be the case if a percussionist violently assaulted the drums. Then there was Amos. He feared nothing and no one to the point of constantly challenging our mother's parental skills. The smaller ones were too little for me to honestly and faithfully share my perception of them as individuals. Individuality was cherished by our parents. Although, ultimately, it was their word that seemed to prevail such were their persuasive abilities. Everything was pondered then talked about. We were always provided with choices so that we could nurture the value of independence in us. That is, unless an emergency required a quick, active response like the day when Amos fell off a tree, causing his broken clavicle to be exposed. I remember his screams of horror to such a volume that I was never able to remove it from my dreams.

My early childhood years in Poland took place in Lodz where I was born, a city located 75 miles or so southwest of Warsaw. I still carry fond memories of those years. We don't often see how happy we were in our past until the future catches up with us. I remember it would not take much long until one day I would read the dreadful sign *Wohngebiet der Juden Betreten Verboten,* "Forbidden to Enter the Jewish Residential Area."

The days were long and warm despite the grim weather outside. Mornings were hectic. My mother had a strict routine to make sure every child would be out the front door at the expected time to attend school. As a rule of thumb, rain or shine, she would find time to infuse us with Jewish values: act with loving kindness, be content, be grateful, be inclusive, be sorry and repent, cultivate friendship and peace. However, those values were already inside us even before she taught them. Mine was a very loving family, I am extremely blessed to be able to say so.

Before the morning rush, my mother would sit with us and sing *Modeh Ani,* "I give thanks to you, Oh God, eternal and living ruler, who in mercy has returned my soul to me; great is your faithfulness." Before washing she would recite, "We praise you, eternal God. Thank you for my body. It is a miracle!" And that's how being grateful was cemented in our souls early in life. She prayed before eating, thanking God for the food on the table. Also, before leaving the house, she touched the mezuzah with her fingertips, which traveled softy to her lips, sealing the respectful kiss as a sign of commitment and faith.

When Ezra reached the age of 5, he began his Torah studies, as tradition mandated. He was brought for the first time to the local *cheder,* a school for Jewish children where he would learn Hebrew and develop his religious knowledge of Jewish life, swaddled in our father's tallit. I was 4 years old then. Invariably, Ezra gave me the impression of an old soul with so much responsibility on his shoulders, maybe more than he could carry being so young. I learned the value of a mitzvah from him. The practice of a good deed as a commandment from God was his daily mission. Observing him, I also learned about responsibility and discipline. I still miss him dearly.

In 1936, he turned 10 years old. Every time we would turn quarrelsome as all children do, he would teach us and guide us to make peace. He would do that with his wise demeanor, which made him appear much older than his age. The disarming look in his eyes was hypnotic. We would cease fire just by staring at it. That year, anti-semitic sentiment was growing like a plague in Poland. I could sense it, despite my young age. On the streets, people would stare at you in disdain. When we were walking home from school, the non-Jews' mean stare had spit in it.

Between the years of 1865 and 1897, the Industrial Revolution in Lodz saw a population increase due to the textile manufacturing that took place there. That prosperity predated me. Back in 1936, my father sold the fabrics business in Lodz, seeking a partner to invest in another enterprise in Warsaw. One winter night, his cousin Aaron came to our home for a quick visit. That's when my father had an epiphany about establishing a partnership with him, which eventually turned out to take shape not in Warsaw but in France. So his visits to Paris became as organic as breathing. Meanwhile, my mother held the family together back in Warsaw.

The years went by. We became more and more reclusive, trying to disguise our Jewish identity. When Ezra was 12, I was 11, Elizabeth was 10, Sarah was 9, Amos was only 7, Ephraim was 6, and the twins Rachel and Leah were 5. Abraham, the last one, was 3. The only thing I recall about Rachel and Leah is that whenever our father gave them a gift, they would insist on having the same toy, the same color, the same size! Besides, they were anything but identical. Rachel appeared more of an introvert than Leah, who always made sure she would get what she wanted whatever it took. My father's business was thriving in Paris. More often than not, his trips to the City of Lights left my mother inconsolable. Gradually, she became bitter and her once cheerful smile sunk into her face until she finally turned dead inside.

During the First World War, the political regime in the German-occupied Kingdom of Poland brought such social misery to the local population. Many Jews were made homeless and forced to dwell in gloomy apartments, causing them to die of hunger and diseases. In 1915, a terrifying phenomenon occurred: the racialization of disease. Although I wasn't born then, its effect lingered over the years. During my time, I can describe how it felt to be looked at with contempt because of my Jewish heritage and how hurtful it was to be considered the carrier of illnesses. We were seen as the threat from the East. Germans fumigated homes, dislodged families and placed them in delousing facilities. This increasing oppression was an act of aggression toward Polish Jews rather than based on any scientific evidence to justify such measures. In their racial theories, it was crucial to protect the *Volkskörper*, "the national German body," from parasites and other pests. As a consequence, a then newly-found lice-ridden disease named "Typhus" was quickly associated with Polish-Jewish factory workers, a statement that German leaders used in order to expel Jews from teutonic land.

In German-occupied Poland, the press wasn't based on facts but on xenophobia. As I found out later on through historical evidence, there were many other infectious diseases coming from rural areas where Jews didn't live. The highly distorted data surrounding the epidemic caused Jewish families much suffering by the hands of the military-occupied land, forced them into homelessness, squalid and cramped dwelling conditions, geographic dislocation, and mass violence. From the beginning of time, we were always hated. Then I thought to myself, "Who would hate a nation who always made the practice of peace and kindness their mission?" Then I cried. Nothing else in the world could have forced my tears to dry. I drowned in them as birds seeking to escape the oil-filled ocean, neglected for so long due to a scarcity of love.

Back in 1936, as my father spent most of his time in Paris, my mother understood that times were changing. We were hiding our identity more and more each day, a fact she concealed from my father every time he came to visit. Early that year, he arrived in Warsaw with a special gift for me. He looked me in the eyes, I could feel the warmth of his tender smile, then he said, "Sadie, I have a surprise for you. It came a little late but I am glad to be able to give it to you now, my princess. I wrapped it up myself!" he said as his smile lit up. A lavender organza fabric embraced the petite black box. Inside it, a pair of blue sapphire earrings softly hugged by dark red velvet lining worthy of royalty. Funny as it may seem, I didn't feel I was put on a pedestal. It was my father's own way of showing how appreciated I was. I recall being in a trance. In that brief moment, the Divine and I were one. Peace and kindness reigned all over us and we could finally be free. He said, "Sadie, these are the most splendid blue sapphires, and you know what they represent?" I was suddenly speechless but I managed to reply, "No." He continued, "From ancient times, people believed blue sapphires were a link to spiritual enlightenment, that it protected people on their journey in life, even in the most troublesome of times. Remember this, Sadie."

That evening, I had an unsettling nightmare. I saw my father disappearing in the dust behind the sound of screaming gun power, which filled the air with menace. I looked up to the sky and there was my mother with Ezra,

Elizabeth, and the twins Rachel and Leah, floating aimlessly like lost feathers. Two of my other siblings were not born yet, which seemed strange to me because in real life they - Sarah and Amos - predated the twins. But dreams are called so for a reason: they lack a solid foot in reality. Contrastingly, I always thought nightmares were a heightened representation of our reality so that our psyche could solve its mysteries by means of association. The old clock startled me to a jolt. I woke up bathed in clammy sweat, and so promptly shaken that it felt like my body was up but my soul was still lying down in bed.

In the morning, my mother decided not to take us to school so we could spend more time as a family before my father had to depart again to Paris. I had the sweetest breakfast that day. I remember noticing my mother's smile returning to its natural source when she gazed at my dad and siblings. The biggest sign of love was evident when my parents resumed their amicable bickering about the smallest of things, from what color they should paint the walls to how to properly place the umbrella by the front door in order to prevent the floor from getting wet and cause a slip and fall.

The breakfast didn't taste like wonderful potato latkes, or crispy wurst, or the sweetest challah toast. It tasted like Paradise! Then came the time when my father had to leave back to France, and our lives would never be the same again. Little did I know it then. There are things in life that others can take away from us but the memories…they persist as a reminder of bliss; at other times, horror. The memories we carry are indelible as we drift away slowly from this perceived reality called Life.

Between the years of 1936 and 1939, my mother formed a close-knit small gathering of Jewish women. She ended up meeting a few of their husbands as well. They met at our home in Warsaw. They read Jewish literature, taught their children good values and the importance of sticking together if harsh times came. They also read, not in front of the children, Nazi propaganda and other literature in order to better study the enemy and increase their odds of survival.

In 1939, I was 12 years old. Being curious as a cat, I sneaked out the backyard where all of the children were playing and overheard the horrors yet to come. That was the first time I learned what hatred felt like, real hatred. The feeling of superiority over others had a low-vibration. It was foreign to me the fact that some people deemed the torture of fellow human beings a justifiable act. Beatings, home invasions, and other atrocities were happening before our eyes. Still, some of us refused to believe it could worsen. As I like to say, "Denial is the hardest drug overlooked by the FDA." People feed on denial until it is too late to change the outcome.

I held the handrail as I eavesdropped. My hands started to tremble in fear. I heard my mother say to her neighbor, "We must figure out a hiding place in case...just in case..." My brain shut off, I could hear no more. I accidentally knocked off the flower vase, which was by the base of the handrail, causing it to fragment into tiny pieces of my traumatized psyche. I silently opened the door under the stairs to hide there until no one was around. My cry was muffled by the wooden walls around me. A close friend Esther said hurriedly, "We must carve out a plan to protect the children. How are we going to do that?" Her words traveled down from my neck to my lower back in tingly mode, and I froze. When my tears subsided, another lady added, "I heard of a boy who was..." She only managed to gesture but not to finish her sentence. So, I peaked out and confirmed my suspicion that all of them understood the meaning of her unspoken words. I waited for an opportunity to escape and rejoin the other kids in the backyard but they were diligently watching their surroundings. I felt trapped. That was the very first time I experienced captivity.

Half an hour later, I heard my mother say, "I have an idea." From that point on, they whispered. My total unawareness of the content of that conversation tore a burning hole inside me. I wanted to return to the children in the backyard as much as I wanted to stay and hear what they were saying. I tried to distract myself by staring at the wooden walls. I then noticed they were mildewed. Their grim surface was not as shiny and polished as it was once when my father spent most of the time with us. My mother had kept those unpleasant details from him because she wanted him to trust that she was taking proper care of her family as any loving mother should do.

One sunny afternoon, she received a correspondence from Paris:

"My sweetheart,

I am planning my return to Warsaw. I was able to hire a trustworthy manager for our jewelry store. He came very well-recommended. I hired him on the spot. I am very happy to say I'll be home permanently because now it's about time for Ezra's Bar Mitzvah. I miss you. I miss all of you. I will be back in about a month.

Our love will never die,

S."

Before his homecoming, Ezra fell mysteriously ill. It became harder and harder to seek medical care without becoming a target to German authorities and their racial hygiene practices. On his way to the restroom, Ezra collapsed to the floor one day. My mother released a deafening scream. I rushed up the stairs and there he was wobbly like a boneless cadaver. My mother kept hidden from my father the fact that the money for provisions was confiscated by the Germans, which placed us a step away from malnutrition. My mother's body, once plump and healthy, became waif-like. She neglected herself in order to feed her children. Unbeknownst to her, Ezra had been feeding his younger siblings when he was given his daily meal portions. I once challenged him about it, since we were closer in age and I felt I could talk to him as equal, to which he replied, "I am fine. Trust me."

When Ezra's feeble body was lying on the ground, my mother sobbed uncontrollably. She turned back to look at me, "Take the children to the backyard, Sadie!" I was about to do so but when I turned my back, I heard him moaning then he made a rattling sound. He looked confused and a shy trace of a smile appeared on his boney face. Then a sigh, longer than Time itself, took him away forever. My mother released a horrible cry of desperation, "No!"

I left the scene. I could still hear her symphony of despair for years to come. It haunted me for an eternity. I rushed back to take a brief moment and ask the children to say a prayer for our family, and for the rest of the world...

CHAPTER 3

Everything is created twice, first in the mind and then in reality." - Robin S. Sharma

The arrangements for Ezra's funeral were never made. When the news reached my father in Paris, he made all the efforts to return the earliest possible to Warsaw. The German military restricted borders so traveling became much harder than before. He couldn't reach Poland in time for a funeral. To make matters worse, no service would take place for Ezra, since German authorities would murder our whole family in case they suspected or merely implied that anyone in our clan had Typhus, according to their distorted agenda "the Jewish disease." So my mother kept silent about his death. She and I buried his small body in the backyard while our neighbor entertained the children upstairs. I was 12 years old when I buried my older brother. I was 12 years old when my world collapsed. And digging my brother's grave was something that hadn't crossed my mind until reality caught up with me and I saw myself in the act.

As the days went by, my parents communicated often. My

father made numerous attempts to go back to Poland but, for whatever reason, he wasn't allowed to return early enough as I expected. The distance between us grew larger. By now, we were living in separate emotional continents. I could only "try" to understand my father's pain. His first born son who was prepping for his Bar Mitzvah; who, according to the rose-colored lenses my mother had placed before him about our actual living conditions, was a healthy boy; and who was soon-to-become a man.

I lost count of the nights when I held my blue sapphire earrings in the palm of my hands and had thoughts of protection. I used to close my eyes, clear my mind, and pray for Adonai to cast away all pain from our lives. Then I reminded myself some people are branded with the sign of sacrifice. Nevertheless, martyrdom is a choice. I choose not to be a victim. I shall never give to others the power of control over myself.

On the same token, I realized how hard it must have been for my mother not to properly bury her first born son, a decision she made to protect the lives of the rest of us. She was so taken by his brutal demise that I don't believe she was thinking in her right mind. I chose to believe the innocent children's prayer was able to lift Ezra's soul on that tragic day and prompt his frail carcass all the way up the sky to enlightenment, as fast and confident as a rocket that never stops. Hopefully, he experienced no pain when he departed this world and was finally allowed to lead the virtuous life he was denied in this existence.

Nazi Poland proved a dismal reality. One afternoon, we received the visit of a couple of family acquaintances, or so we were told. In fact, they were members of a more serious discussion group that held discussions on what they knew was happening in Lodz. On September 9, 1939, the first *Wehrmacht* troops arrived after the Polish resistance surrendered to the Nazis. I realized then we were already under complete German control in Warsaw because the same events that occurred in Lodz, such as the germanization of the Polish culture, had already taken place there in Warsaw. They eliminated everything written in Polish. The biggest blow to Polish culture was the elimination of the press written in Polish. Language is a representation of its people so when they replaced all writings to impose their own language, that brutal imposition was an act of violence in itself. It had the power to crush people by erasing their culture, as a consequence, their very existence. And that was one step away from murder. Not only did the Germans remove the most symbolic aspect of any culture but also they forced Poles to work for meager wages so that they would only survive dependent on very basic needs such as food, shelter, and clothing. Mind you, and I am a witness, food was not proper for consumption, shelter meant living in squalor, and clothing was reduced to mere *schmatte*, or what the goyim would call "rags."

As the chatting became more intense, the gathering commented on the deportation of Polish Jews to Germany, and on something I couldn't understand at the time namely *Intelligenzaktion*. Simply put, it meant that the Nazis deported Polish intellectuals to concentration camps in Germany. The ones who weren't expelled, ended up ruthlessly murdered in the nearby woods. The news struck me so hard I felt fatally bitten by a wild cat as I were the only meal available. Why is it that the first tactical thing to annihilate a people's identity is to remove any trace of their culture: their practices, religion, the local press, language, and the local intellectuals? Maybe we are all animals after all, in the sense that we forget that nature isn't apart from us. We are nature. As animals, we can also smell fear, anxiety, and are able to use that piece of information to our advantage, despite the fact that we are the only beings who create history. Yet, instead of learning from past mistakes, we keep perpetuating them. Consequently, that illustrates how eliminating intellectuals is a strategic tactic to remove any thinking heads that could potentially challenge the enforced system. Any military regime, be it a dictatorship, the Third Reich, a military *coup d'état* - all synonyms, by the way - relies on banishing intelligence. This military tactic eliminates any peaceful roundtable discussion based on intelligence, facts, and proven scientific evidences. The truth does not matter to them because they are able to fabricate it by imposing their distorted data. It's all oh-so-easy to point a finger at someone else and blame them for something they haven't done. By blaming others, no one would pay any attention to the detractor. So the truth is shifted very carefully. Reality can be shaped by making a decision on either doing the right thing or misusing the truth to manipulate people's perception of it. Aggressive regimes shamelessly enjoy washing brains because denial is still a very powerful drug. To face reality, one needs strength of character, which is something many people lack. Soon after, the chats revolved around children who were snatched in Lodz straight from the hands of their parents and sent away with no information on their whereabouts. They simply vanished.

The following morning, my siblings and I were playing in my bedroom which had become the only chamber in the house close enough to fake a decent room. On the Southwest corner, my favorite blanket. Right next to the base of the bed was my trunk with the few books I owned, which I reread countless times. Sarah opened it and said in her high-pitched voice, "Can you read us a story, Sadie?" "Of course" I replied. She added, "Where's Ezra?" My words dropped from my mouth downward to my stomach. Elizabeth stopped singing and asked, "Yes, mother told us he went to Paris to spend some time there before his Bar Mitzvah. Is that true? If it is, I want to go there to stay with father too. Why can't I?" Elizabeth's once jolly face now had a question mark stamped on it. Then I said, "Why would you believe mother would not speak the truth to you?"

It's unfortunate that I was forced to become an expert liar at a young age. Guilt lingers in your epidermis, eating you inside only to burst like blister when reality changes, despite people's inability to understand where the outburst originated. Such is the role of tension in your system, it simmers quietly and under pressure.

"Why don't I read you a story?" suggested Sarah. Despite her deaf left ear, she retold a whole Jewish folk tale verbatim like the great reporter she was. I miss my sister Sarah so much. And to think that those moments of closeness, with my siblings beside me, helped me stand stronger on my own feet later on. Their laughter and their cute faces were souvenirs I would keep forever in my soul. However, the merriment of a full house would be gone soon under the grim shadows of a dark present.

The subsequent days proved my theory. Mainly when I realized the gatherings at my home were secretly held at odd hours and the children and I were told to "Just go upstairs and stay in your room!" I recall one night around 2 AM when a suspicious knock on the front door woke me up, the others remained asleep. The knock had a cadence that seemed to conceal a secret code. After a pause, I heard it again. Soon, I heard my mother steps descending the stairs to open the front entry door. I sneaked out of my bedroom. I could tell Elizabeth was dreaming of a beautiful place, her face filled with joy and blissful warmth. The others slept like only innocents do. I concluded not to wear any type of shoes so as to protect my invisibility. I then proceeded downstairs quietly holding the now tainted handrail. Mother was in the kitchen, the light remained off. A candle was the only detectable witness to that conversation. When I thought of the children who were kidnapped and taken away from their parents in Lodz, my birthplace, I was convinced I had the right to know what would become of my siblings and I.

"Name is Heinrich, as you can verify from my papers. Last name is also German so it wouldn't be any problem when…" My right foot slipped on the wet floor, for water had been dripping from the exfoliated ceiling paint for quite a long time, for we had no funds to repair it. A squeak was all it took to send my mother zooming to the hallway to find out if anyone was spying on them. Thank Goodness I had time to hide behind the old piano nearby. She resumed her meeting with Heinrich. From this point on, I was so fearful she could find out I was eavesdropping that I decided to tiptoe to the stairs. I was fully alert like a rodent in the light, just in case I had to rush upstairs without uttering a sound. Heinrich handed her a bunch of papers that looked like German official documents. I could guess by looking at the stamps. She signed the papers and gave them back to him. She sighed. He said, "Don't worry. They are safe with me." His words chilled my spine. "See you Friday. Thank you." She paid him well, which came as a surprise to me. He then left unnoticed into the foggy night like a wandering ghost.

I could not possibly fall asleep the whole night. I thought of my brothers and sisters playing happily in the backyard and of the times when I read to them. The memory of Ezra's burial was still fresh as well as the episode when I had to lie to my siblings in order to keep them from the truth. My body went numb, soon my head followed.

One day, a scrawny man came in through the kitchen door. "Mrs. Goldmann? Heinrich sent me." "Children, go play in the bedroom now!" She made me an angry gesture, indicating that I should take them. I caught a glimpse of his frightful visage. He had a scruffy salt-and-pepper beard, green piercing eyes, and a left-sided smirk. She looked uncomfortable before him yet she seemed aware his presence was a necessity. "Come on, let's go play in the room" I told the children then looked back swiftly and was able to witness him giving her letters that seemed to have traveled from afar. She gave me a threatening, disciplinary stare. I shrunk in my humility, turned my back and headed toward my bedroom to join my siblings.

The following morning, we received an unusual visitor: Heinrich. He looked very well-put. He wore a respectable suit, tie, polished shoes, and an even shinier demeanor. Anyone would have mistaken him for a gentleman. I still couldn't trust him. "Sadie, children, please come downstairs to the living room," my mother ordered. "You see all these letters? They're from our relatives in America. You will be staying with them. Wait for mom and dad to join you. Ezra will be there too." When she mentioned Ezra, I could smell deceit in her words. She passed the German documents to each one of my siblings but me. "That's not my name," said Amos. "That's not my photo," added Elizabeth. My mother told us that Ezra and my father were waiting for us in a beautiful land called America where we would meet our cousins, uncles, and aunts, people we had only heard of but hadn't met yet. The letters were real, and the fakes documents - I learned much later - looked real as well.

Hours later, my siblings and I were separated forever and I would never see them again. My mother and I dressed them up spotlessly so as not to raise any suspicion. One day she revealed to me she had arranged fake German documents for the children so that Heinrich would pass as their German father and make sure, at least according to his promise and fat payment, that they would be transported to our relatives in New York. Before they left through the front door, I noticed their faces in slow motion. I suppose my mind was capturing their smiles ominously for the last time. Their eyes glistened as the sunbeams kissed them gently. I uttered a heartfelt goodbye.

The rest of the afternoon evaporated into thin air like the vanishing clouds in the sky, making way to a hopeful new start. Around 6 PM, I was sitting on father's reclining chair in the living area. My mother was frying something odorless in the kitchen. The sound of deep fried food coming from the kitchen worked as a threatening swarm of flies, as if the fizzle of pouring acid dissolved the children's faces from my memory when they were taken away. Albeit their smiles remained an indelible souvenir that would torment me perpetually. If anyone asked me, I would never say anything against my mother. She did what she could with the hand she was dealt. And her cards weren't great! Who was I to judge decisions that were made under such circumstances? By embracing this conclusion, I was able to find peace within myself.

A week later, Esther burst in with startling news: my father was finally coming home to us! My mother took that verbal report like a sharp dagger into her chest. Then she let it out, "What should I tell him?" "The truth," I said. Esther held her shoulders, inviting her to sit down. She poured water into the kettle and made some herbal tea. "Here, this should soothe you, Ruthie." The warm herbs calmed my mother's nerves. For the first time in years, she looked younger, relaxed. Esther caressed mother's hair maternally. My mother raised her eyes to look at her in gratitude. "Remember we must meet soon to discuss the hiding spot. It's not safe here anymore, Ruthie." Esther's eyes rushed toward me then moved rapidly back to mother. "It's about time we built us a shelter," said Esther. My assumption about their open communication before me led me to believe they considered me mature enough to grasp what was happening in the world. Was I?

At night, my thoughts concentrated on the children. If anyone asked me how I survived the horrors, I'd be inclined to answer, "Because I love Life!" I don't think there's a need for me to apologize for my oversharing. Suffering, pain, love, faith, hope, everything is part of life. Then I'd ask you the reader, "Despite everything, isn't Life just gorgeous?"

For quite a while, I dreamed of Abraham's 3-year-old naïveté. Although I couldn't tell much about his character since he was too young for it to have developed yet, I can say his gaze encapsulated life and death. Its purity cleansed my soul every time he observed me stoically.

The temple of my childhood, of my cheerful family years was doomed. An unforeseen glare coming from outside almost blinded me. Then a blow so loud that almost rendered me deaf, followed by silence. My heart didn't beat anymore, or so it appeared. I saw the whole living room wall collapsing before my eyes. My mother stood there in shock. Esther hugged her, forcing her to look the other way. I noticed her dress getting wet from the tears she shed. Our home had been bombed. How would I rejoin my father now? When Esther managed to bring mother back from her state, we decided to gather only the most relevant belongings. I rushed upstairs against my mother's advice to recover my blue sapphire earrings, somehow they represented me just like my father once said. I lied to my mother saying I really had to go to my room to recover something important, I omitted to her what it was. We wrapped ourselves in torn blankets and headed out the door.

Warsaw was a pile of scattered debris. Whole buildings were falling into ruin. People screaming on the alleys. Behind the tallest construction I could see, a former one-story deli, another glare. Esther pulled me closer as to indicate the direction we should go. Between signs that read *Juden* and desecrated stars of David violated by the Nazi swastika on them, I forgot who I was. My existence was instantly erased like Rothko's blurred masterpieces, only my emotions were left behind just as if his vivid colors heightened even more what I was experiencing. I let out a piercing cry. Esther slapped me to wake me up from my shock.

Minutes later, we took a right on a dilapidated former pharmacy and we managed to arrive at Esther's house. Her husband Ira received us as if we were their close relatives. I reconnected with my family values, and regained hope that soon my father would be able to see me again. "Maybe my siblings were safe in New York," I insisted on believing. We sat down to say our prayers. It was the loneliest meal I ever had so far. We all glanced at each other in humility, as if reluctant to be noticed by the other. Then we ate the watery soup, devoid of any garnishing or vegetables. We held each other's hands, lowered our heads and our silent prayer intimidated the loneliness. Before long, there was peace at the table.

CHAPTER 4

 Learn to value yourself, which means: fight for your happiness." - Ayn Rand

Centipedes, mosquitoes, spiders, maggots, well-nourished rats, every sort of critter inhabited the basement where we would soon build our shelter. It was wet, stuffy, slum-like, and there was sewage water leaking from the wall coming from above. I dreaded that place. The sun came up. Ira showed us the spot where we would start our construction. He disappeared in a dark corner. When he came back, he was holding a bag of cement. He pointed at the sand, binder, and water. Esther, Ira, my mother and I started preparing the mixture and worked incessantly, for our very lives were endangered. We waited patiently for the cement to cure so it would harden, for it was obvious the weathered basement itself wasn't the strongest of places to begin with. Notwithstanding, it was the sole "option" we had.

That was my first lesson in masonry. I recognized the insouciance on my mother's face as she wiped her salty perspiration off her forehead. We all labored for a good cause: our survival. Just as soon as the shelter was finished, Ira shared that France was taken. It was the beginning of 1940. My thoughts went to my father. I had been busy and forgotten about him whom I was supposed to rejoin in Warsaw. How would he know we were staying with Esther and Ira? Who could be our emissary to inform him of our whereabouts?

The basement was muggy, nauseating, oppressive. I felt sticky all over my body yet the dampness was rather intensified by my mind's orchestrations sometimes. Esther and mother went upstairs to fix us lunch. Ira left to purchase a few goods for the days to come so that we wouldn't starve. When Ira came back, he walked down to the basement where I was ordered to stay and wait. I darted toward him, "Please, do you have any news about my father? It's been a long time. Is he in Warsaw?" Ira assured me he would update me about the matter. He gave me a fatherly look. I attempted a smile but my mouth was too weak to force its muscles to accomplish the task. He patted my back. "Come. We must eat."

At the dining table, silence prevailed. Those glacial instances during meals turned me resilient. Consequently, I became unable to shed a single lonely tear. Soon, lunch was over. Esther asked me to check the pantry to see if we needed any food, cleaning items, and so on. "Sadie, I want to teach you how to be independent just in case we're not here to care for you tomorrow," she told me. My mother nodded. Those words stroke me as fast like lightning, for I was then cognizant of my soon-to-be parentless condition. I had no emotions to spare after that realization. All I could hope was that my mother wasn't planning to abandon me.

The shelter we forged could fit about five families with two children each. That accomplishment made me proud of my contribution. The living room table clock announced 7 PM. Esther, my mother and I were cleaning the house when

Ira stormed in with more families to join us in the shelter below in that repulsive basement. "Sadie, can you take them downstairs?" he asked me. There were three families to share the house with us. We Jews learn early in life the value of charity so it didn't seem unusual to host and provide for others in the same situation or worse. I indicated the basement door and led them to the shelter. They assembled their belongings, hardly any.

Joseph introduced his wife Abigail and their two children Adam and Jonathan who were 3 and 2 years old, respectively. "These are our friends Thomas and Edna. And this is Ethan, their son," said Joseph. As all of us became acquainted, I couldn't take my eyes off Ethan. He was about my age and had the brightest green eyes I had ever seen. "Nice to meet you..." he told me. "Sadie," I answered. The awkwardness grew between us like bliss. He was slim, olive-skinned, intelligent, and so on. I could spend all eternity describing his qualities. It was so silly I often caught myself being so self-conscious. In our hideout, there was another couple Noah and Martha. They were childless newlyweds whom we considered the non-conformers of the bunch. Gradually, we managed to accommodate everyone into their own little nooks. At night, I used to sing a Yiddish lullaby to Adam and Jonathan until they fell asleep. Every time I sang to them, Ethan and I exchanged looks. Then the glacier inside me melted like a running stream.

Two nights later, a loud explosion was heard outside the house. We all rushed to our shelter. "Stay quiet everyone," advised Joseph. He held Abigail who in turn held their two sons Adam and Jonathan. The oldest couple Thomas and Edna looked at each other with impending doom. Noah and Martha remained nonchalant to, as they would say, "just another bombing." Ethan and I were the only ones who could still carry the fire of hope in our eyes. His smile just beamed which stirred some discomfort inside me. "Why are you smiling?" I challenged him. I then looked at my mother. She was not the strong, elegant, and hopeful lady she once was. I thought how hard it was for me to look at her and recognize what she was before. Her sadness robbed her of her confidence. Esther made most of the decisions then, not as an authoritative figure but rather as someone who saw in my mother a person who was losing her identity.

A few minutes afterwards, German soldiers busted the front door to raid the house. Luckily, they weren't able to hear a single breath downstairs. We held ourselves together silently as we heard the Nazis breaking the furniture in the living room, in the kitchen, and we couldn't utter a word. Pride was an expensive commodity!

When we were able to return upstairs, Esther realized the kitchen had been completely damaged. She understood that it would be impossible for her to cook again, much less for so many people. The weight of the world fell on her shoulders as she slowly sat down, her head slightly askew. I walked over to her and placed my hands on her shoulders. She turned back to face me then kissed my left hand in gratitude. The family I had lost I somehow recovered at Esther's house. My brothers were gone but I found a brand-new close-knit community and every single one them was as loving and caring. Such is the way the Universe works!

Ira left with Joseph, Thomas and Noah to seek provisions to feed their extended family. Meanwhile, Esther, Abigail, Edna and Martha attempted to improvise a way to prepare food as soon as the men returned. Ethan entertained the two brothers in the living room with storytelling. I went upstairs to see what I could find for us and I stumbled upon a book. The cover was sturdy. It was made of leather and the paper was rough. There was a makeshift bookmark. I opened the page, removed the bookmark. That specific page was almost blank, except for a sentence that said, "The minds of others are an uninhabitable land." I rushed downstairs with the book under my clothes and read it alone near a candle-lit corner. The pages confided in me the reason why Esther was childless. After several efforts, her doctor had told her she would never be able to bear a child. One day, she miraculously became pregnant but an accident put an end to her dream. The pages told me that one summer when she crossed the street downtown after grocery shopping, a large vehicle hit her throwing her against a street light, causing a miscarriage. She was never the same after that accident. Although every one around her felt her devotion, all the love her child was denied she selflessly bestowed upon others.

Ira, Joseph, Thomas and Noah returned with limited ingredients for a decent meal. Ira knew a former Jewish baker and he used to make the best challah in town. However, after his deportation, his wife kept the family alive by learning some of his recipes, except for the challah. She believed the challah should remain his specialty so she refused to undertake the challenge. We all sat upstairs in the kitchen at a rickety table close to a more sturdy one so we could accommodate each member of our little community.

Next day, the routine unfolded in the same fashion, except that that time I stayed in the basement reading the book instead of going upstairs. Ethan noticed my absence. While I read, his voice served as a backdrop for my literary discoveries. I was so absorbed in the stories, I hadn't noticed he stopped singing for the two children. He was standing by the base of the stairs leading to the basement when I was aware of his presence. He moved in slow motion toward me. My eyes tried to escape his but I was hopelessly trapped in them already. In spite of the setting, the soft touch of his lips against mine gave me freedom. All of a sudden, the whole basement turned into a beautiful tree-lined boulevard with birds singing and friendly clouds drawing a friendly smile in the sky and the sun shone so intensely I became the light. I caressed his hair. He wrapped his fingers in mine. What he didn't realize was that he had restored my joie de vivre, something I promised myself I would never lose again.

The men were back. That time they brought another rescue, a 17 year-old girl named Miriam. She was nine months pregnant and the imminent delivery posed a threat to our safety. "We couldn't leave her in this state," Ira told Esther, trying to persuade her to let Miriam stay. Esther held Miriam by the right shoulder, pulled her closer and walked into the house with her. Looking back, I believe Esther may not have had her own children but she was everyone's mother. And how lucky we all were!

Life crushed our spirits harder and harder. One early morning, around 5 AM, the men left on their daily quest to provide for our clan. Hours later, however, only Ira returned. The Nazis had captured Joseph, Thomas and Noah. Their women were inconsolable. Ethan's eyes saddened so I ran my hand over his hair to show him my support for having lost his father. Thankfully, the others were oblivious to our mutual affection. Ira and Ethan were the only men in charge of providing for us from then on. The grieving wives chopped the vegetables Ira had brought home. When I finished eating, Ira asked me to check the living room to see if I could find his phone book. As I searched the drawers, he told me, "I heard of your father. He will arrive this coming Tuesday around noon. I can give you further details later," he said. "You will see him again," he said. I lacked words to describe how that last statement affected my soul.

Before dinner, Miriam went into labor. Esther ordered the other women to gather warm damp towels and sterile items. My mother resumed her servile position as her lust for life had vanished long ago. "Take Adam and Jonathan to play in the living room, please," Esther asked Ethan. When Ethan, Adam and Jonathan left the room, Edna added, "She's bleeding too much." "Please, I don't want to die," cried Miriam. "We need to take her to the basement and put her in bed," said Esther. "But there's no bed that can hold her in this state," said Martha as Miriam's body moved seismically. Esther answered, "We'll figure this out. Downstairs, I say. If she stays here, the Nazis will find us."

The baby was born on a cold winter night. His nest was a humid, unsteady wicker crib I handmade. When I looked around, I observed every crevice of the decaying refuge we had built for ourselves. That site was not fit for a child to be born in. The baby cried at birth. It was a girl! She had the most gorgeous honey-colored eyes and looked just like Miriam. They both rested together for a while. Miriam swaddled her daughter with a ragged blanket. "My baby, welcome to this world." Miriam was so feeble she couldn't produce any milk to feed her child so Ira offered to get some milk for the newborn. He returned with better provisions that time. We all had a nice meal. Soon after, Ira became ill. He had a few red dots on his forearm that indicated he had been bitten by a critter, maybe a spider. The baby remained serene as long as we still had milk for her. Ira's arm throbbed as his eyes bulged in pain. Martha yelled uncontrollably, "We're going to die." Esther held her by the arms and slapped her to wake her up from her nonsense. "No, we are not," Esther added.

The next morning, we had no more food available. Ira was feverish and the women voted for Ethan to be the one in charge of food. Despite being one year older than me, Ethan wasn't as savvy as I was but he was as brave. He left to meet the contact from whom Ira usually obtained our resources.

When the baby woke up, no one could stop her piercing cry. She screamed as if all the maladies in the world were tormenting her. She just wouldn't stop, and we were all fearful of getting caught. Miriam held her close and tried to give her some peace. "Do you hear the footsteps," whispered Miriam to us. In an attempt to save her daughter's life and that of others, Miriam smothered the poor baby's body so firmly that little angel stopped breathing. When she realized what she had done, she drowned her agony into the river of sorrows yet without making a sound. We all remained inaudible for quite a while until Ethan came downstairs. "It's me," he told us. We all looked at each other. The noise upstairs weren't the Germans, after all. "Where's the baby? I brought milk." Miriam sobbed. Her misery was joined by her guilt.

Shortly, we heard footsteps pacing upstairs heading toward the basement. "Into the hiding spot," Esther ordered. We had built a door with a fake exterior so the Nazis would mistake it for just another wall. We rushed to the shelter but our bodies lacked the vitality to succeed. A Nazi officer grabbed Miriam by the neck, almost suffocating her. She managed to bite him and free herself from his hands. Abigail, Adam, Jonathan, Edna, Martha, Miriam, Ethan and I were held prisoners. That Tuesday, when my imagination had previously made it so real I would see my father again, I lost my freedom. I also lost my second family when we were forced to travel away toward the unknown.

We all live in this dome we call Earth. Whether we make it a cage or a welcoming place relies solely on each individual, which is to say either we get along, or we don't. When we don't, my God, it's a Greek tragedy in five acts!

Whenever the military vehicle drove over a bump, we were jerked left to right. There were no windows. Our destination was kept an enigma. It didn't take long for the driver to come to a stop. Two officers swung open the back door. We were forced out to the train line. The women were separated from the boys. That was the last time I saw Ethan. I waited patiently beside my mother. Esther, Abigail and Edna were sent to another line to wait for the next train. I saw Esther cry for the very first time a good real sobbing as if she had given up all faith in her survival. My mother and I were shoved into the train. The steam blended with the snow that fell unhurriedly outside like a foggy dream.

The snow flakes seemed to caress the air, falling like lost feathers in distress and moving side to side with no final destination. I hugged my mother and gave her a kiss on the forehead. At that moment, I was the adult; she, the child. As the locomotive moved, I approached the window to take a last look outside. The weather was dreamlike. I couldn't tell the snowflakes and my tears apart, as the latter were also freezing. I noticed a man starring from a distance. He rushed toward me then I focused on him. It couldn't be. It was my father. "Sadie," he screamed. He ran so fast he got much closer to the window. The tip of my fingers managed to touch his hand then they separated. An officer immobilized him, he tried to escape and the officer covered him in fuel. They set my father on fire as he screamed in agony.

The train moved away faster as I caught a last glimpse of his burning body. And I thought to myself, "Evil tries to mock us when it should mock itself. Evil is ridiculous and shameful. Kindness is beauty. It takes effort to be mean, but it's easy to be good."

CHAPTER 5

It was 1941 when I was sent to the camp. I was 14 years old then. During the trip, I had a nightmare. I saw my father ablaze. He smiled as if he were freed from this world's troubles. Then I heard my mother scream as Miriam held her dead baby. The fog covered those horrendous scenes. Ethan came out of the mist to kiss me only to disintegrate in thin air. I was suddenly teleported to my happy home. I ate a challah toast and cheerfully enjoyed my siblings as they played. Their laughter was so contagious. The whole scene faded swiftly and I was left alone, buttering the bread.

I woke up startled. My mother was trembling in her sleep. The snow insisted on following us along. I found my inner peace and learned the power of non-reactive behavior by observing the snowfall. It served me well as a teacher. Then I thought about how we Jews were being targeted. I told myself, "Whenever people try to blame you for something; the problem is in them, not in you. They must take responsibility for their wrongdoing. Many times, aggressors are brave to hold a gun to commit a crime but the mere act of taking responsibility for their actions scares them to death simply because they're weak. You, Sadie, are strong!" I kept those words as my mantra throughout my life, to always remind myself of the power of resilience.

Auschwitz was the biggest concentration camp complex. There were three main camps; one, specifically for murder. The entrance sign read *Arbeit Macht Frei*, "Work makes one free." Needless to mention, all the work was performed by the Jewish prisoners while the Germans used us as forced labor under the false Aryan superiority. The three camps were Auschwitz I, Auschwitz II, and Auschwitz III. I was sent to Auschwitz II, also called Birkenau. It was located near Krakow, I later learned. Little did we know that one of their way of killing us was forcing us into extremely hard labor, which was their initial tactic to get rid of us until they came up with better solutions to suit their sick ideology.

Women, men, and children were assigned dorms. Inside them, there were bunk beds and, as I remember well, there were so many people in them which made each dorm not only overcrowded but overflowing with human souls. As prisoners, we had to wear striped pants and jackets. It didn't matter whether the shoes fit you or not, you would wear them just the same. Why bother changing the clothes when it was time to sleep since the great majority of us wasn't able to have a peaceful rest until the following day when we would wake up in the wee hours to be coerced, used, humiliated, and degraded performing hard labor? The dorms didn't have any windows so we felt the weather, hot or cold, due to the lack of insulation. We would use a bucket to relieve ourselves. The bunk beds were in deplorable conditions and we were squeezed among 400 people or more, eating food that was rotten. Sickness was a daily companion, and so were hunger and dehydration. Whenever one of us refused to eat the spoiled food or drink the filthy water, a barbaric soldier would come and beat us to a pulp. I couldn't possibly cry because my eyes refused to believe in what was happening before them. Some skilled workers were assigned as barbers. But who would want to cut the hair of those who tortured your women, your children, and you? It turned out that the lighter job ended up being of a bigger moral sacrifice than other assignments. They kept a storage overflown with our belongings. Clothes, shoes, children's glasses that were shattered just like our souls were. Those piles of belongings were mere numbers to them because we were all branded as cattle, literally and figuratively. We were stripped off our individuality. If the reader can think of a better way to disenfranchise someone's identity and feelings, would please let me know…

The following day, I woke up, pushed myself to eat the rotten soup and drank the water. I realized then there would be no sun, real or imaginary, during my stay in that horrific place. When it was time to be assigned to a job, I was designated to shoeshine. I would have to spend my entire days polishing Nazi shoes until they could see their faces reflected on them. During my shifts, and despite a job well-done, a certain general would intently spill beer over their own shoe as a subterfuge to slap me and say, "Look at what you've done?"

Some of us worked in coal mines, dug tunnels, cleared the snow, or were sent to work in dim-lit factories to forge more weapons of destruction. There were no limits to their vicious ambitions. "There's insanity in megalomania," I thought. Good luck to those who tried to escape. There were a handful of watch towers and enough guards with rifles in their hands to shoot at the sound of a floating feather. Many prisoners committed suicide by jumping to their deaths toward the electric-charged barb wire fences. Death seemed the only escape from the subjugation they were under.

Days came when I experienced famine and hunger because I had thrown the food and the water away cautiously and kept the look in my eyes gnomic so as to not raise any suspicion to the German guards. My answers were short. I only had "yes" or "no" for words. Will the reader please forgive my verbose rambling, for I spent too many years in monosyllables. I speak from the heart not the pithy mind, as I share my life with you.

The savage guards seemed to be chosen according to how ruthless they would execute the regime's blood-thirsty agenda. I spent my ravenous nights thinking of my family and how happy I was until the war made me a destitute. I was disgusted by the treatment we received. One week later, I was reassigned to perform hard labor like most of the prisoners. Until then, I could tell how much time had gone by because I developed the habit of marking the walls wherever I was stationed so as to keep track of time.

I met Christina De Castro, a Sephardic Jew. As we were both hostages in the same dorm, Christina and I used to spend the nights sharing our memories and comparing our Jewish traditions. She sang in Ladino, a mixture of Hebrew and Spanish with hints of Arabic and other influences, as I recall her saying. To me, there was passion and longing in those words. Although the lyrics were indiscernible to me, I used to close my eyes and dream of green pastures, vineyards, the breeze blowing my hair wildly and Ethan's face approaching me for a long-awaited kiss. Whenever she sang, I reconnected with my inner peace. I was immediately sent flying up above, and I floated like large-winged birds do when they look like they are immobile in the sky. That feeling would last long until I fell asleep. Her melodies were my sleeping pill then. I was surprised about the differences between our backgrounds as Jews. Christina told me that Sephardic tradition allowed her to eat *Kitniot* during Passover. I told her we were forbidden to eat those foods - rice, corn, millet, dried beans, lentils, peanuts - and she looked at me surprised. Then she described me her favorite Chanukah foods like cassola, bimuelos, keftes de espinaka, and I told her about my mother's famous latkes. We laughed at our deep-fried shared experiences. Then we dreamed about a more abundant life. She told me her mother named her after her aunt who couldn't have children. "You can't name a baby after a living relative," I told her. "Yes, you can," she replied. Apparently, there was more dissimilarity in our Jewish heritage than we could have imagined. Christina and I bonded, as we learned to embrace our differences. She was vibrant, I was shy. She was red, I was blue. I perceived her narratives as injections of joy straight into my veins. She stared at me with her big brown eyes, soon we would have no secrets between us.

Our days filled up with longing for brighter days. I stopped marking the walls because I had a gut feeling my life was about to change. For better or worse, I did not know. Approximately a month later, the guards brought to our dorm Izabela Argentari, a Romani young girl our age. One day, one of our roommates, an elderly lady called Katya came up with an epithet for us: The Three Musketeers. We busted laughing because it was so true how close-knit the three of us were. During our nightly storytelling, Izabela described her place in Romania before the Nazis raided it. She told us she had six siblings and belonged to a tight community of Roma people. "Gypsies?" I asked. "No. Roma," she replied. She explained that "gypsy" was a derogatory term that meant how others saw them as thieves, murderers, children kidnappers, and dangerous. She enlightened us about the centuries of persecution suffered by her people wherever they went.

"But why?" she asked. Due to our obvious lack of response, she added, "Because we have freedom. We don't abide by society's rules. We believe freedom is only free if it is unrestricted. If we were to adhere to other people's commands just to fit in then we wouldn't be free, would we?" Those words fermented in my head like a yeast-filled concoction the whole night.

In the morning, I was still awake thinking about her observation on what it meant to be free. "Still awake, silly," Izabela asked me. "You made me think a lot yesterday. About freedom," I said to her. "Freedom is a beautiful word to describe a condition not everyone possesses. Whenever you tell society they're not free, they gaslight you. It's easier for them to believe themselves free than face the fact that they conform. It's also shocking to them when they see a true free person enjoying life with good food, dancing, doing business - not in a brick-and-mortar but on the streets, anywhere! The freedom of coming and going as you may please scares them. Close your eyes now, Sadie. Think: I AM FREE!" I repeated that affirmation for a while until it was time to resume our daily toil.

The moon shone brighter than usual that night as we marched to the barracks. Before I reached the door, I saw a glare as bright as day coming from behind one of the warehouses. "Hurry, go!" ordered the soldier. When the guards shut the door, we heard an altercation right outside then the sound of a slap and a spit. Suddenly, they reopened the door and shove in what appeared to be another roommate. Everyone was petrified so we kept to ourselves. The night regained its tranquility, and we were finally able fall asleep.

At dawn, the new roommate shook like a leaf. I noticed his manly bone structures yet soft gestures. When a clumsy roommate was using the bucket, she dropped it and woke the newcomer up. It was a man! I suspected the guards had made a mistake because men and women were housed separately. I couldn't help but notice a downward-pointed pink triangle on his chest. He had also a capital letter "A" on his arm and the number 175.

"Nathan," he said gently, hoping we would not feel threatened by his gender. Nathan smiled at me, I returned the gesture kindly. It was Sunday, he told me, so we had no work to do and the reason he was there with us women was that the Nazis wanted him to spend one day with the "weaker sex" because of his sin. He explained that the pink triangle meant he was identified as a homosexual. The number 175 came from the German Criminal Code and had that same connotation. "What does the capital 'A' mean?" I asked. He shook his head, refusing to answer. Nathan slept the whole day curled like a baby. Before the moon came up, he was abruptly taken away from us, lingering like a question mark in our heads. To my dismay, they also took Izabela and Christina away.

That morning, I was sent to help excavate a big pit outdoors. The sight of my older brother Ezra spooked me. We were a total of ten prisoners working on the ditch. In the end, they sent us back to the barracks. Then a deafening noise hurt my ear drums. I rushed to peak through the crevices on the wall. Numberless corpses made their final journey into their graves, unemotionally dumped by a truck. In a little while, a bulldozer pushed the soil and covered the rotten carcasses. Before meeting their deaths, their bodies were already in such bad condition. Many had diseases that caused them to smell pungently. I would never forget the scent of dead flesh. When I looked again with more intent, I saw that Christina and Izabela were among the victims. "My sisters," I said to myself.

As I marched on my way to another assignment, a German lieutenant kept staring at me while driving his automobile. His eyes seemed friendly. He had very short black hair, bushy eyebrows, no lips, and handsome. I didn't feel threatened. The vehicle came to a stop. He stared at me with more determination. Then he drove it before us to stop the march. "What is this female doing here?" he confronted a guard, referring to me. "She is needed at the hospital, these are the orders," he added. The Lieutenant took me by the arm away from the marching crowd of skeletal laborers. When we were far enough to be safe, he winked at me. I tried to allow myself to trust him. "Lieutenant Johann. *Wie heißen sie? What is your name?*" he asked. "Sadie." I was told to climb the back seat then he drove off fast.

The wind in my hair brought back the past. Except that time I was optimistic. Maybe my intuition was right, my life was really changing. I was hoping, for the better… I thought of Christina's stories about her happy days in Spain, signing, dancing, and simply loving and being loved. How similar she was to Izabela, maybe because Sephardic Jews also had a Romani influence in Spain. I differed from them because my joy was introverted. Still, mine was as vibrant inwardly and that's the reason why three of us bonded. I touched my forehead and made a promise that their memories would remain with me forever.

CHAPTER 6

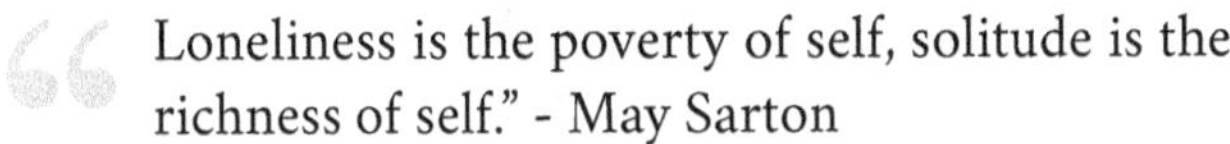

Loneliness is the poverty of self, solitude is the richness of self." - May Sarton

There are three types of people: wolves, foxes, and hyenas. Wolves crave attention. They use manipulation to lead the masses "the hyenas" to destroy beauty and reign in a kingdom of dirt. I fall under the fox category. Foxes realize the schemes wolves come up with but we are smart enough not to play their game and to refuse following hyenas. Foxes understand the importance of non-reactive behavior. Foxes hunt. Hyenas resort themselves to merely mocking others who are different, those like me who beat to their own drum. Every time there's a dissident, wolves push hyenas to scorn, laugh, torture, and hurt in every way possible those who are just trying to lead their lives. One thing wolves don't realize, or maybe refuse to acknowledge, is that foxes are much smarter and we use our brains to escape their stratagem, intellectually.

I started my new assignment as a nurse in 1942. I worked from 7 AM until 9 PM assisting the other medical staff in providing care for German soldiers. At first, I thought I found a way to reconnect with my evolving self through my daily reading. Johann allowed me to have a few books, which he brought to me by disguising them in a leather folder he always carried. One day, he showed up with notebook lined papers and encouraged me to write my observations on the treatments. Later on, I would find out what he really meant was for me to write about "the soldier's health improvements, not about everything." I had mistaken his generic assertion as a sign to document everything I experienced, I was wrong.

After a few weeks, I recovered my sense of time. There was a calendar on the wall within the facility. I was forced to work on Shabbat. That was the way they used to belittle my heritage. One afternoon, a German guard came in with his forehead oozing blood. I heard later that morning that he was drinking with fellow guards and beating a scraggly Jewish man when he accidentally slipped and hit his head on a vehicle then fell into the pit used as a mass grave. When he arrived, his forehead was bleeding profusely and dirt covered his cheeks and mouth. He laughed in the most grotesque way. The other two guards who had carried him in left. I cleaned his face with antiseptic. For a good while, he ceased his laughter and stood there quietly receiving my care. When I was done, I approached the door and signaled to the guards who waited in the hallway that he was ready. I then walked back in to remind him of his dismissal. He then placed his filthy hands under my clothes. "Stop," I said. I can't possibly bring myself to repeat the vile words he said to me. The doctor took an eternity to show up but fortunately Johann came in to drop the books and to collect the last one he had lent me. He instantly told the guard, "What are you waiting for? You are dismissed. Go!" Johann told him. I understood my objectification by the guard. I was a number, just one among so many.

On Friday, September 3, 1942, I was raped. It happened around 8:55 PM when I was heading to the backroom where they allowed me to sleep so that, in case they needed me to wake up at night, I would be available 24 hours a day. I remember how uncomfortable the tiny cot was. I would unfold it every night and refold it in the morning. Falling asleep was a challenge because the cot was so fragile. My body kept reminding me it would break at any minute. On the night I was raped, I wasn't able to feel the cot's discomfort. I wasn't able to feel anything. And I dreamed of Warsaw, and the cold winters, and the warm home I had with my parents and siblings. My thoughts traveled to Christina's Spanish pastures and colorful Sephardic music, which was very similar to Izabela's culture as well. Then I told myself I wasn't alone, that the situation would pass, that I would one day rise to a new reality because... I was a fox, after all. I was a survivor, and no one would break me.

When I woke up, I was bleeding from my anus. Johann violated me so roughly I was not able to walk for two days. They placed me in the backroom, lying on the army green cot, which brought back the remembrance of that tragic night. The sterile facilities contrasted with the way I saw my body, which felt filthy, broken into, then discarded like an object. Like a number! Izabela once shared that she already knew what she would face by the hands of the Nazi, not because she was a Roma but because, on her way to the camp, she was transported on a wagon only fit to move cattle and many died on the journey. Similarly, I taught myself to embrace that recent symbolic death so I could overcome the present and secure myself a future. In order to survive I needed to be stronger than ever, way beyond all the pain.

Many German physicians as well as scientists believed in

racial hygiene, even before the Third Reich. So, with the prospect of jobs in research, they welcomed eugenics as way of securing a career and supporting the regime's focus on biology and hereditary. The idea of the perfect human being was born. There was neither room for those born with disabilities nor those from an inferior race.

A wounded General arrived once. I was on watch, it was around 10 PM on a Saturday. I heard the backroom door open. They brought me to assist him because the other "stupid nurse" was ill, they told me. General Otto was a blond, square-jawed, tall, menacing German, what eugenicists would consider a perfect example of a healthy, superior male. Johann burst in with jealousy but held himself back because of his lower military rank. Otto's eyes traveled all over my body. A slight touch wasn't required for me to feel penetrated again. After I treated the General's arm, he left the room with a satanic grin. Johann observed attentively. The General returned and leaned on the door. "Where are you from?" he asked me. "She's just a filthy Jew," said Johann with hopes of persuading the General not to pursue me. Successfully, I rarely saw General Otto back at the infirmary again. When Johann and I were left alone in the room, he slapped me. I slipped and fell. Then he kicked me in the stomach viciously.

The circus of horrors continued only to include more stories of brutality. The routine between the backroom and the infirmary proved claustrophobic. I heard of the experiments they were conducting on prisoners. One day, a healthy female Jew was brought in. At that point, I was made assistant to their cruel endeavors. The doctor cut the woman's leg open, injected her with bacteria to study a new medicine response. Working at the infirmary made me aware of sulfa drugs testing, bone-grafting, and nauseating researches where they infected the victims with typhus, malaria, tuberculosis, and other diseases. At other camps, I overheard one day, they conducted experiments on hypothermia, which caused many Jews to freeze to death. At Auschwitz, they carried out gruesome experiments to secure the mass sterilization of the inferior races, the Jews, the Roma, those born with disabilities, and other minorities. Many victims suffered indescribably, were mutilated, permanently disabled, and there was a metal box, as I recall, where they dumped their limbs as in a butcher shop. Fortunately, I wasn't witness to those harsher cases of anger, violence, hatred. The bone and joint transplants, the freezing tests, the mass sterilization just to make sure we wouldn't reproduce! Yet they were the ones who shouldn't be allowed to reproduce their Evil, in the first place.

I thought about my mother, my siblings, whether their legs had been cut off, or poisoned, or were made ill with yellow fever, malaria… I thought about the high altitude experiments in Dachau, when I overheard from a nearby conversation one day, where prisoners were subjugated to about 65,000 feet low-pressure chambers in order to study how high German pilots would be able to parachute. The outcome was sure death. "But the real dead were them," I thought. They were dead in their hearts and their souls. To test sulfa drugs, I heard they rubbed dirt, broken glass and tetanus bacteria on victims, leading to horrifying endings.

Lying down in the army-green cot, in the dark backroom, I documented everything I heard until the morning when I finally understood the reason why Johann had given me the lined papers. "What do you plan on doing writing these lies?" he asked. I did not react, nor answer. He set fire to my notes yet my eyes were the ones ablaze, fixated on the dancing flames of the papers. "Red and blue, just like Christina and I," I thought. "Next time, I will send you to the…" he continued but my mind refused to register the completion of his sentence. Physically, I was present but not spiritually.

Another time, a man in his thirties, thin as a rake yet washed to the point I'd consider him sterile, was brought in. Jozef, a Roma male. That was one of the worst days of my life. I was coerced to hand in the scalp to the doctor who removed Jozef's organs without any anesthesia. Jozef didn't survive the procedure. Without any justifiable reason, the doctor then castrated him. Jozef's body was sent to the huge dumpster to be covered by damp soil. My feelings were boiling. I couldn't stand it anymore. When I received the news that Jozef's body was buried, I lash out at Johann. I slapped him, push him, punched him in the face, and sobbed uncontrollably. Right then, he looked afraid of me. I grabbed a chair and threatened to kill him. General Otto appeared and ordered the guards to immobilize me as I screamed, yelled, and cursed them.

I was sent to a grisly room with rusty nails on the walls that prevent me from sleeping. The ceiling was low and water dripping so slowly from above that I could literally keep track of the drops as a means to tell time. I lived in that room for quite some time. There was a gap under the door big enough to push a bowl of dirty soup under it - once a day. Whenever my body claimed itself as worthy of rest, I would wake up with bleeding hands because I had used them to protect my neck and face, for it was so tight and the nails were in such close proximity as to jeopardize my life.

When they reopened the door, my eyes almost went blind. The light was so bright I thought I had died. I woke up back to reality when a guard pulled me out of the solitary by the arm and threw me on the hallway floor. It was a curious feeling being confined in there, as I recall, because I never felt lonely. There was solitude, yes, but not loneliness. I used that time to gather my thoughts and come up with a plan so I that I would secure my posterity. I told myself, "You are a fox, Sadie. No one can break you."

They returned me to my position as a nurse. I thanked the universe I hadn't been sent to die as a number. Tragically, one day when I was about to administer a medication to treat an officer's wife, two German guards brought in what appeared to be a person wrapped in a frayed bedspread with blood stains. When I finished with her care, she got up. At the door, she fired me a look I will never forget. Another nurse Sarah came in to aide me. We slowly unwrapped the bedspread. "Nathan," I said. He attempted a smile. His face was bruised, his right leg injured badly. "Hi, princess," he told me. In 1942, I was 15 years old but I felt much older. Hearing someone call me "a princess" seemed odd as it didn't match the Sadie I was then. Along the years, Sadie evolved into several versions of herself in living each day. "Sadie, it's almost time for me to go. Will you manage?" Sarah asked. "Please, you can go," I answered.

Nathan expressed his anger toward the regime. I advised him to save his energy to recover, to survive. He told me about other atrocities in Dachau. Stories about an SS doctor performing artificial insemination on prisoners by putting animal sperm in them and terrifying them about their future offspring. "There they also forced gypsies to drink seawater to see if it could be drinkable. I hate them," he shared. I wiped his injuries with antiseptic. His clean face revealed a handsome man with kind yet sorrowful eyes and a rough life. "What does the capital 'A' mean?" I asked but he remained nonchalant. It hurt me to witness his tortured soul being denied respect due to his sexual orientation. He told me he had survived for a while by hiding he was a homosexual. He then finally explained what the capital 'A' meant.

He told me the Nazis hated homosexuals. "Men who have sex with other men?" I asked, confused about the term. He explained that society at large thought of it as a disease and that many families disinherited their homosexual relatives, others sent them to mental institutions. And that it was considered unnatural! "Is marriage natural, I ask you, Sadie?" I didn't have words to reply. "No, marriage is a construction, a fiction built by society in order to control the survival of species. It's not natural because animals don't get married. God, or whatever is up there, did not create marriage. Man did!" he shared. "Those who hate me are those who fear being the same way. They just cannot tolerate the possibility of nurturing in themselves the same attraction," he added. I looked at that beautiful man whose soul seemed so huge as to embrace the whole world, and I couldn't allow him to reinforce the hatred for which he was being targeted. "I don't recommend you love them. But don't give hate any fuel, Nathan," I begged him as I wiped his forehead. He continued,"In nature, some species have relations man-with-male and female-with-female. Would you say animals are unnatural because of that?"

We spent a while talking about nature, God, society, love, hate, music. When we finally stopped to say a prayer, peace and love prevailed in the room. "To whoever is suffering in these horrendous times" we said in unison.

Minutes later, we heard steps in the hallway. "Quick! I have a plan for you," I told him. I showed him the narrow passageway leading to my backroom. "Wait for me there," I suggested. At night, Nathan and I carried on our discussions on numerous topics. He told me he was a musician who played the violin, the piano, and knew how to sing. I hummed a tune, muted enough to attract any attention from the guards. "You can't sing, Sadie," he laughed. "But I can teach you," he added. I realized I hadn't smiled for a long time, far too long. We exchanged glances. What a beautiful soul he was! When he slept, I wept.

In the morning, after he helped me refold the cot, he would hide all day until I came back to the room after my shift to share with him the little I had to eat and drink. As a fox, I paid careful attention to where the food and beverages were stored. Eventually, I was eating much better and the water I drank was as clean as my consciousness. Nathan was looking a lot better then. His face regained its vitality, his eyes were glowing with life just like a heavenly apparition.

When they changed the night staff, our worries increased. The guard on duty was industrious. It took two of his shifts for Nathan to be found in the backroom. Soon, they found out and took him away forever. My abduction went unnoticed by the ones in charge. Johann had carefully hidden me in the back of his vehicle. I ducked there surrounded by the ammunition and camouflaged under a heavy army green canvas. When he drove away, I realized I was his hostage again.

CHAPTER 7

The loftier the soul, the greater the challenges and darkness surrounding it, like the most valuable pearl which is set in the largest encasement." - Rabbi Menachem Mendel Kotzk, Lubavitcher Rebbe

I turned 16 years old on August 16, 1943. Exhausted, the years of abuse took a toll on me as I was heading to the unknown again. Would that mysterious destination be better or worse than my previous bondage?

Johann pulled me off the vehicle by the arm. He had blindfolded me for the whole trip. As he forced me to walk, I stumbled upon what seemed to be a broken sidewalk then was violently pulled into a building. Inside it, Johann removed the cloth that surrounded my head. The lobby was somber, dim-lit, and had very stark furniture that imposed austerity. He took me up the stairs, which sent my head to a dizzy haze. Upstairs, we stopped before a black door. Johann pushed me in, causing me to land on the floor. The bedroom had minimal furniture: a bookcase with volumes and volumes on Nazi themes, a dressing table with an oval mirror near the window, a solid wooden armoire, and a handmade embroidered rug decor with a swastika above the bed. There was a gramophone on a bedside table with a golden brass horn and velvet green cover so the 78 RPMs wouldn't scratch. Only Classical Music was allowed in his record collection. Classical, grandiose, austere!

Johann left. He locked the door behind him. The claustrophobic environment where I was would require me to take prescription drugs in my later years. I was locked, robbed of my freedom. Again!

The days progressed as I scrubbed the floors, polished the furniture, polished Johann's shoes, ironed his uniform, cooked with the help of a small stove he brought to the room so that he would keep me under the radar. "At least, I ate the same quality of food he had," I thought. The windows were also hermetically locked, in case I nurtured any lofty dreams of freedom. Every morning when he left, I would look through the window glass and my imagination would take flight just as a bird does. I would land on a tree branch then look below, as if observing humanity from a higher vantage point. I thought how much Nathan must have suffered for his sexual orientation. Nathan taught me about art, music, and life. He also opened my eyes to what was happening at other camps. I thought of Christina and her people when I remembered that the Nazis forced the Roma prisoners to drink seawater refusing to feed them. The dehydration made them lick the floor in search of a single drop of fresh water.

Johann returned at the end of day, locked the door behind him, removed his boots then threw them at me, gesturing me to clean them. Resiliently, I followed his order. "We are in Berlin now," he said. My imagination went way back to Nathan's stories of gay Berlin. I had never been to Germany before, so the only reference I had was Nathan's storytelling.

He told me once about the center of gay life in 1920s Berlin around Nollendorfplatz, the Eldorado nightclub, the male and female impersonation shows, and how free everyone felt to be able to express themselves as they desired, free of hate and persecution. Reality changed as soon as Paragraph 175 was penned.

In my four-cornered room, my living coffin so to speak, Johann ordered me around. Nothing short of perfection, at any task I performed. Maybe he was punishing me for hiding Nathan, thus, jeopardizing his position and safety somehow. I do not intend to justify his actions by any means but I noticed he became more demanding each day, as if he felt he needed to punish me for something. "I had to arrange our move here because of you. If I stayed, they would know about that scum you hid in the backroom," he said. I was right, he was punishing me. "In Auschwitz, four large ovens were built to burn corpses. Be glad I didn't leave you there," he said. Hearing about not one but four large crematoria was enough for me to experience the searing pain myself. Johann described the crematorium routine to me in detail. Prisoners walked into a room to undress then walk into a lethal gas chamber where they met their deaths. Later, the corpses were incinerated in the large ovens... I did not speak to him for days, as I recall.

One day, a knock at the door. A manly female came in to instruct me in German. She wore an olive-green pleated skirt and the top looked like a trench coat cut in half with a mannish navy tie. Her hair was also masculine, and so were her mannerisms. "Sit!" she ordered. In the subsequent weeks, Johann ordered me to learn German. Helga, the instructor, got in the habit of hitting my hand with a metal ruler whenever I made a grammar mistake, or my accent wasn't perfect enough. She also made me kneel on seeds for hours until my German became not good enough for a foreigner but nothing short of perfect for a German. Helga scarred me. Her eyes invaded my entire body, making me self-conscious, violated. Her ruler went up my skirt once and I slapped it away. She then slapped my behind with it dominated by a twisted pleasure, which I didn't have maturity enough to grasp at the time.

Helga was hired to germanize me and Johann instructed her to dye my hair blonde in the process. In case she would suspect his actions, because to her a Jew would never be as superior as her kind, Johann had told her that his intentions were to destroy my identity by making me more German-like. His attraction and repulsion toward me confused me greatly. As much as he was the one who abused me viciously, it was also due to his actions that I wasn't dead yet. Nonetheless, I never granted him the right to torture me or anyone, ever! Instead, I chose to believe the universe kept me alive for a good reason. My mission wasn't accomplished yet. I had to survive to tell the world what I experienced, to try to make the world a better place, to bring the message of peace, to make humanity more humane!

One day, I followed Johann's orders to dress as a good German lady. He took me for a ride in his automobile. In the car, he told me, "You should pass as a German. Good job removing your accent!" he told me. We stopped by a nondescript establishment, he jumped off the car and went inside. From the interior, he kept watching me through the window. He brought beer and other spirits, sat in the driver's seat and drove off with me. His demeanor was shivering. Was he planning on murdering me? If so, then I had to come up with a last minute survival plan.

He drove to a deserted wooden area. He got us both drunk then kissed me. The disgust in my eyes, the stink of alcohol. I laid there motionless as his lips tried to forced themselves against mine. My body didn't feel alive, it felt like a corpse then. "You don't want to kiss me?" he said then slapped me. I stood there in defiance, staring at him without blinking. My lack of motion cut off his aggression by its roots simply by not reacting. I felt like a harbinger of peace and resilience. I refused to become his equal!

He drove away with me. His drunkenness caused us a car accident. His car hit a wild animal and we almost died. He drove home back to my confinement. Helga arrived immediately after us. The glass from the vehicle was encrusted in my whole body. I was in shock as Helga sadistically removed all the glass off my arms, legs, back, chest... I didn't feel any physical pain but, emotionally, I was shattered just like the glass.

As I polished his boots the day after, Johann told me, "We are very lucky." I was confused. "When I arranged our move here to Berlin, I managed to be selected for the *Sicherheitsdienst des Reichsführers- SS*," which meant he started working for Hitler's secret service. He explained he was assigned to manage a recording room in the basement of a brothel in Charlottenburg. The madame was a former street worker. She helped Jews flee to England with corsets with her business money stored secretly in them. So she was given the "option" to collaborate with the regime and let "us" run her brothel. He added, "The women were carefully chosen as the embodiment of perfection to feed us information on world leaders and SS officers, in case there's a dissident. You could pass as a German. If you don't behave, I can arrange with the Madam to give you work there." He held me by the arms with both of his hands steadily. "As a prostitute."

The following days were as quiet as a tomb. Helga wasn't needed anymore as my German language skills neared perfection. The more I "seemed" germanized the more vicious Johann's attraction became. He started to gaslight me often to instill doubt in my soul. He gaslighted me about beating me with a broom stick, hitting me with a phone cord, scratching my back with his nails, and about the day when he ran his fingers through my hair and banged my head against the wall. He also denied calling me a burden, a disgrace.

When he was absent for work, the long hours by myself allowed me to create a plan to escape. I started working on impersonating a German man like Johann. Nathan's stories of gay Berlin taught me a great lesson. He used to describe how women impersonated men at the cabarets in Nollendorplatz. In a week from then, I was able to pass as a male. The last thing to accomplish my self-training was to somehow obtain fake papers to make my plan feasible.

Johann ordered me to wear drag one evening, which caused me some alarm. We drove to Charlottenburg to his workplace. "You are a German officer now," he told me. The brothel received all the high rank members within the regime as well as diplomats and royalty from other lands. "You will get your fellow Germans drunk. Encourage them to drink." We entered the white building. I was shaking inside like an earthquake afraid of blowing my cover. I followed his instructions and suggested a general to drink more and more. When Johann signaled to me to persuade the General to take a specific lady of the night, I heeded. The General was later discovered as a British spy and was later killed by gunshot by the Gestapo. "Who will take this beautiful lady here?" asked an intoxicated royal. "He," Johann said, pointing at me. I was disoriented by his words. I was a lady, after all. That would blow my cover. "Come over here, handsome man. I have a fuzzy surprise for you," told me the German prostitute while rubbing her hand on my thigh. Ah, that sickening Johann! For the first time, I felt a bitter taste inside me as hatred raised like bile from my stomach up to my mouth and my lips tasted salty like hot blood. Hate tasted like blood, I realized.

"Stop!" Johann barked. "He's too drunk to get it up," he added. I swore to myself that would be the very last time that nasty thing, for he wasn't a real man, would belittle me.

We arrived at the airless room he called bedroom, I burst into vengeful tears and lashed out at him. I punched and kicked him with all my strength. He close his hand and hit me so hard I flew against the armoire. I grabbed the bucket from under the furniture and threw the urine at his face. The anger grew in him. When he rushed to attack me, he fell and hit his head on the corner of the bed. He suddenly didn't get up. I stared at him for quite some time, waiting. My prayers had been heard when his vital signs told me he was gone.

Time was a ticking clock that pushed me to make a life-changing last minute decision again. In the morning, he wouldn't show up at his desk. That meant I would be discovered, and killed. I spent that night cleaning the mess. I took all the money he stored inside the gramophone. I wrapped his heavy body with the swastika decor from above the bed then dragged him into the armoire. I then worked on my Johann impersonation before the mirror, headed out the door on the tip of my toes, and purged that version of Sadie forever.

CHAPTER 8

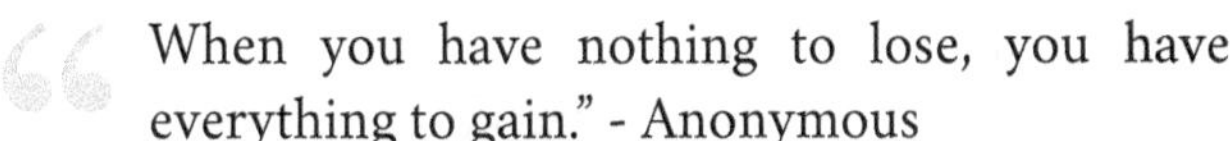

When you have nothing to lose, you have everything to gain." - Anonymous

Living with snakes teaches us how to produce antidotes. I was on a train, looking out the window, disguised as a German civilian. I had decided not to wear any uniform because the camouflage wouldn't hold for long so I resorted to passing as a nonmilitary subject. I was only 17 years old then.

I would like to keep this chapter short since I do not recall the entire trip. At best, I remember stepping off the train in London and rubbing both of my forearms in the River Thames as a symbolic baptism. The benthic creatures at the bottom of the river made me dream of a brand-new start. In my vivid imagination, I thought of the gas chamber victims as a ballet of dead flowers whose souls attempted to climb up to the top of an invisible mountain, grappling each other, unsuccessfully.

CHAPTER 9

Life is what matters, and even death was once life. Life is in everything. That's why it prevails - over war, crime, injustice, everything." - Anonymous

In early 1945, The Soviet Army liberated the Auschwitz camp and its subcamps. Lamentably, the SS units held a westbound March to Death with over 55,000 prisoners before the soviets arrived. The war was over, finally!

The streets of London concealed my tears, which merged with the daily precipitation. Although England had accepted us Jews in its territory, the anti-semitic attitude straggled back, refusing to rub elbows with us. I heard Londoners say, "The Jews are to blame for the war." How can anyone blame the victims for the abuse they suffered? Was torture, by any chance, justifiable!?!

During the war, the East End Jewish community was subjected to bombings. There were hate signs everywhere. The fact that the authorities preferred to remain blind to facts was alarming. One day, I came across an abandoned house with a friendly reminder that said, "Britannia rules the waves - yeth, but we rule Britannia." Those were verses from a "patriotic" song originated from a centuries-old British poem by Thomas Arne, which was associated with the Royal Navy and British Army. Ah, the military again!

I found a job position as a maid in the fancy Mayfair neighborhood through a Jewish community center in the East End, where only Jewish women completely desperate for work met. I was issued my domestic service visa. My new occupation had me work from 8 AM until 11 PM, however, I would have the "luxury" of a half day off once a week, which prompted me to voice my rights saying, "I am only one person. This seems to be a lot of work, more than one single person can endure" to which my employer replied, "If this does not suit you, I shall send you back to Auschwitz."

The manor was enormous. The ugly subservient uniforms and the pretentious superiority of the British suddenly didn't seem to differ much from the treatment I previously endured. Although Britain had opened its arms to us, it's a misconception to believe we weren't given a cold-shoulder.

The manor was adjacent to Hyde Park. Contrastingly, the beautiful gardens near the property remained a sight to be enjoyed from a distance. Still, on my days off I went out to watch the birds. Most often, it rained so my planning went down the drain in a spiral of lost hopes. Oh, the isolating feeling of what it entails to be an immigrant in a foreign land, hearing an unfamiliar language, thus, not fully integrated! I saw myself as a bird who chirped a different tune - which was long lost - a melodic and warm song others weren't able to reproduce. That feeling turned my confidence inward to then choke it in my self-conscious bubble.

After a while, I gave up hope I'd see a sunny day. I bought an umbrella to call my own and became a member of a club for Jewish maids. I realized that, in spite of my erudite upbringing and real life experience, I would never be hired for a better position rather than the backbreaking job I was expected to do. Wherever you may go in the world, what locals will never understand as part of the immigrant experience is that we immigrants are reduced to expandable jobs. Despite possessing the potential to be the best candidate for a higher position, we are downsized to do low-paying jobs, recruited as a number!

On the other hand, I also heard lighter stories at the maids community group. A 2o-year-old girl told us about her matchmaker whom she met through a cousin. "It is *beshert*, it's meant to be," she said, gladly holding up the photograph of her fiancé. I used her cheerful account to amuse myself a little in order to recover the guilt-free laughter I once lost.

When an upcoming wedding turned things hectic in the home, I had to wake up at 6 AM and was not allowed to sleep before 11:30 PM. My 18-year-old body aged 20 years or so in a month. Any sign of eye or body fatigue would cause the lady of the house a stir to which a solipsistic treatment was all she deigned to offer me.

A month went by. The wedding took place at the grounds of a property in Gloucestershire. After the successful celebration, a 41-year-old British aristocrat Sir Archibald Taylor arrived to have dinner with my employers. Everything had to be meticulously arranged, ordered, placed. The menu consisted of 11 courses: oysters à la Russe, cream of barley soup, poached salmon with white wine sauce, filet mignon, glazed roast duckling with pear sauce, red punch, grilled squab, asparagus creamy salad, foie gras, chocolate ice-cream, assorted fruit and cheese. Courses were brought to the table one at a time, as per the lady of the house choice of *service* à la Russe.

During the posh dinner, Mr. Taylor fixed his eyes on me the entire time. Awkwardly, I did not feel uncomfortable as his gaze was elegant and friendly. "If you allow me, how did you find such lovely help?" he asked the hostess. "Well, she is not precisely very efficient at her job. She was recommended..." she answered without much explanation. "It appears she is performing her duties pretty well, it seems," he added, looking at the hostess in defiance.

I enjoyed witnessing that scene where someone stood up for me. Minutes later, Mr. Taylor pulled me gently to a corner of the living area. Near a massive blue ceramic vase with a tall plant, he said, "You may call me, Archie," and he smiled. "I shall see you..." he said while looking at his little black book "Tomorrow?" I insisted I worked on Saturdays to which he replied, "I will have it arranged that you see me tomorrow."

The following day, Mr. Taylor came by in his white Rolls Royce to speak to my employers. I escorted him down the hallway straight to the library, as per their instruction. The silence was grave-like. At the end of their conversation, I was fired by the lady of the house then to my alarm rehired by Mr. Taylor. "You work for me now, Sadie," he told me. Mr. Taylor coldly accompanied me to the car then he drove away. In the vehicle, he shared, "Do not be concerned, you are safe in my hands. I fancy you. What are your thoughts on marriage?"

Archibald married me on June 22, 1945. As a new British citizen, I fantasized about the freedom I waited so long to experience. Notwithstanding, British society would always give me a certain look to make sure I was deliberately put back in my position as an outsider. Since I came from a middle-class background, I lacked the sophistication that belonged so easily to the upper class. I was constantly reminded to sit a certain way, eat with the right utensil, behave like the other ladies, that is, to blend in, to conform, never to stand out. My identity was once more at risk. My individuality, my thoughts, my tastes were disregarded as plebeian.

I gave birth to Harold on July 4, 1945. He was a handsome blue-eyed, blond, and active baby boy. During the pregnancy, I did not suffer at all. The delivery was easy. However, Archibald's drunkenness increased. He was the meanest when intoxicated. I dreaded him whenever he came home late at night and tried to force himself on me with his sexual advances, from which I often managed to escape. One night, he stayed with me at home. When he noticed I had thrown away all his liquor, he rushed to the library to obtain more of his hidden whiskey from under the upright piano stool. He drank and drank and drank, becoming totally inebriated to the point of collapsing on the library floor. That wouldn't last long.

Archibald got up on his feet, flew to Harold's bedroom and removed him from his crib. "Stop it! You'll hurt him," I said. He held Harold so strongly I was afraid he would break the baby's fragile bones so I grabbed baby scissors and poked his hand lightly so that he would release Harold. In a fit of anger, emotionally charged by the alcohol, he grabbed the scissors and attacked me. He aimed at me unaware Harold's brain was his center target. I then held my baby firmly and turned my body, allowing myself to be stabbed violently in order to protect my dear Harold. I ran to the contiguous room and called the police. Archibald was let go due to his influence as a member of the upper-class. Later, he blamed me because he was "forced" to pay a heft price to be released. From then on, my nightmares returned to stay.

Months later, Harold turned a year old. I spent his first year protecting him from his incapable father. Archibald aged briskly. One afternoon, I waited until he left to attend a meeting somewhere. His favorite part of the house was the library for two reasons: that's where he stored his liquor and his personal, secret papers. The previous day, I hid behind the curtain, unnoticed, so I could spy him and find out the safe combination. Next day, I was able to open it for the first time.

Inside the safe, I saw our wedding document, his bank statements, and his inheritance. I read the whole afternoon, for he wouldn't be back until late. I learned why he chose to marry me. It was not because he nurtured any kind of feeling. His inheritance papers revealed that he could only keep his wealth if he got married, stayed married and produced a child, specifically a son. I realized I married a narcissistic, manipulative brute under the initial disguise of charm and elegance. He had played his role oh-so-well to victimize me and my son Harold, respectively. Archibald also wedded me because I was an immigrant. No fellow British woman would ever take his disruptive behavior but a lost immigrant in a foreign land like me, on the other hand, wouldn't pose any threat.

Looking back, I did try to love him at first. Initially, I thought of him as kind but his entitlement and arrogance caught up with my projection of who I thought he was. I was seeing an idealized version of him, not the person he actually was. When the veil of deceit fell off to the ground, which caused his camouflage to go uncovered, I learned not to seek neither validation from him nor respect because that day would never come. In reality, I only existed in his world to make him feel better about his nasty self.

Empaths try to understand until they are forced to stand under!

An automobile roared outside the window. I rushed to place the papers back into the safe in the identical fashion as he left them. I then locked the combination, adjusted my messy hair enough to be able to feign calmness, and fled the room.

"How was your afternoon?" he asked me, way under the influence. "I read. It was a delightful read," I replied with a mischievous grin.

From that point on, I regained my strength. The faith I used to have, tripled. He was at my command. If I threatened to leave him, he would lose his inheritance, something out of the question for him. The sweet feeling of playing dumb to wolves and hyenas! A strange rush of adrenaline took charge of my body, revitalizing it entirely.

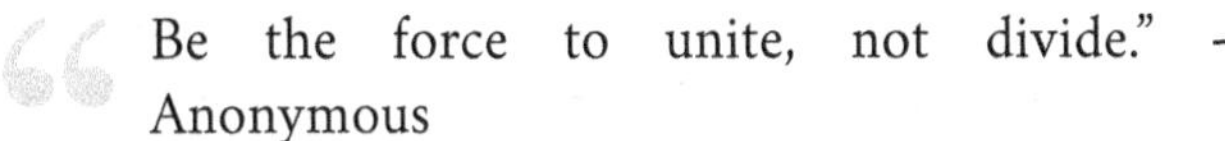

CHAPTER 10

Be the force to unite, not divide." - Anonymous

My mind is as sharp as a razor but my heart is as fragile as a crystal. A year went by since I flipped the script on Archie. Whenever he made an attempt to control me by depleting me from my self-confidence, I counterattacked by placing a mirror before him. His weaknesses scared him so. "It seemed easier to project them on me and downgrade me in order to elevate himself," I realized. From then on, I spent plenty of time devouring the whole library collection as fast as I could.

I mastered my skills at rubbing elbows with British society and soon was able to beat them at their game. After all, their self-professed good manners originated from other cultures. Eating with a fork was introduced by Catherine de' Medici, an Italian noblewoman considered the most influential in 16th century Europe, who followed what was already a common practice at the tables of wealthy families in the Middle East and the Byzantine Empire. Furthermore,

Catherine de Braganza, a Portuguese noble who became the Queen of England, Scotland and Ireland after her marriage to King Charles II, was the single person responsible for the introduction of the habit of drinking tea. During her life in England, the British treated her horribly due to her Roman Catholic roots. The so-called "British" sophistication came from other cultures yet the British were the ones who, along with the Germans and the French, were the Barbarian peoples in previous times. Their persecution of Arabs, Jews, and other nations proved again the theory that Archibald Taylor projected onto me his lack of sophistication, his weaknesses. Moreover, blaming "the other" has always been a military tactic. My intention is not to ignite a war but simply to call it for what it is. From the beginning of times, Mediterraneans were the most developed culture in humanity, and so were the Middle Eastern, the Arabs, and us Jews. So, why so much hated against us? If the Italians hadn't taught the British how to eat with a fork, they would be still eating with their hands like a brute. And if the Portuguese hadn't taught them the habit of enjoying tea in a sophisticated manner, they would not look upon everyone with such superiority. My intent with this exposition is not to encourage animosity among cultures, it's exactly the opposite! I wish society at large would accept foreign cultures. Instead of bullying other nations, claiming foreign discoveries as their own, why not acknowledge other people as equally worthy of compassion and respect?

I attended soirées, opera engagements, and theatre plays with Archie because I felt the need to entertain myself. That served me as a much-needed break from my real life concerns. As a married lady, I couldn't just go out by myself, or maybe I hadn't found a way of sneaking out unnoticeably then. Harold was kept at home with a nanny, an old hag who wore a mole for make-up and never smiled. I often times was truly convinced that she lacked teeth only to realize one circumstance she had them but her character was just sour.

One evening, Archie and I went to a ballroom. "Would you fancy a dance?" he asked. "I'd be glad to," I replied. We waltzed along to the sweet melody of violins. It felt like heaven! After all, it was all pretense and I had learned the British game very well by then. Pretend, Sadie, and you will rise!

As we danced, I caught a glimpse of a young, handsome fellow who was sitting alone near a shadowy corner. He was mysterious, dark-haired, attractive. When the waltz came to an end, I excused myself to Archie so that I could go meet the ladies in the other room. Archie disappeared behind a server, probably on his way to gulp down his liquor and take a puff of his maduro cigar. Unsupervised, I took the opportunity to walk over to the young gentleman. And a gentle man he was!

Spencer introduced himself to me. "Would you fancy a dance?" I invited him. Our bodies moved with synchronicity. The chemistry between us made me sweat a little. "I need some air" I said. "Shall we walk?" he said. We walked to the enormous, half-moon shaped balcony. We were the only ones there, except for the moon itself for witness. "'Tis so bright tonight," he said. I bowed my head with a little girl smirk. My heart was pounding. My thoughts fluttered like a monarch butterfly; yellow, happy, in trance. One of the staff came by. "Oh, I believed there was no one at the balcony. The doors seemed slightly open. Please, excuse me." The tall staff person returned inside to his duties. I then ceased the right set of circumstances and kissed Spencer. He returned the kiss more passionately. In a trice, the moon ceased to exist, and so did the stars, the sky, the Earth, our woes. When I woke up from the reverie, I wrote my address on my silky lavender handkerchief and handed it to him. "Come see me next Sunday, my husband leaves for the club all day. The nanny is off. No one can disturb us." Despite his surprise, he looked at me and the trust was mutual. As we heard the French doors quivering again, he hid the address behind his pocket square. Archie walked toward us. "I felt dizzy. This gentleman brought me outside for some fresh air. What is your name, sir?" I said. "Spencer," he replied. "I appreciate your concern, Mr. Spencer," I said carefully not to raise any suspicion.

Spencer arrived on our date punctually. That day marked the dawn of a torrid love affair. I had decided I was worthy of love, respect, and to be the lead character in my own life. Since Archie had his mistresses, I would have my gentleman lover. Spencer was a talented artist who restored damaged paintings for well-to-do patrons of the Arts. He took me to his dusty flat in the outskirts of London to show me his studio, and we made love near works that, despite the similarity, rather looked like Picassos and Mondrians.

"I would rather see your work," I asked. He gave me a sad look as if he had given up on his potential. "I paint no longer." "Why?" I insisted. He dragged himself to an armoire, opened the double door bathed in paint splats, and revealed 45 masterpieces he created. "'Tis not worth a pound," he added. I was mesmerized by how much talent he had. I wasn't projecting because I was infatuated or maybe in love! I had undressed myself of any biases before I examined his paintings. He truly deserved to exhibit at a Museum.

Those Sundays made me bolder. Soon, I decided to make the trip to his flat. I called Harold's nanny so she would work on Sundays. Unbeknownst to me, my decision of keeping the nanny also on Sundays raised Archie's suspicion.

Spencer gave me painting lessons at my request. Soon, we created artworks in the nude after making love. He preferred using an easel, I'd rather put the unprimed canvas on the floor because it allowed me more freedom. Archie stayed at home for two Sundays while the nanny cared for Harold. He guzzled down his scotch. I could smell it in his breath, when I arrived from Spencer's.

"Where has you been?" he asked. "I've been taking painting lessons. Actually, I have an exhibition coming up." It was true I arranged an exhibition with my work and Spencer's at a small venue Downtown. "You are invited," I added. He took me by the arm, "You appear very jolly recently," he said. I released myself with energy. His nonverbal threat shook me a little.

The exhibition took place at a former warehouse turned gallery. A factory had closed so the building was sold to a some philanthropist Lady Estella who enjoyed discovering new talent. "I'm so nervous," I told Spencer. Prior to the art show, Archie had told me he wouldn't grace me with his presence, which made me comfortable to talk to my love freely. "Who is that gent staring at my work? He's been there for 15 minutes, at least," I asked Spencer. The man walked toward us. "Are you the artist?" he asked me. 'Would you accept my invitation to show your work in Paris. Phillippe Beauchamp, enchanté." "She will accept," Spencer answered swiftly. Archie appeared intoxicated by the entrance. When he spotted me, he came in enraged. Spencer noticed his state and told the marchand, "Allow me to show more of her work, would you fancy some wine?" Spencer took the marchand away to protect my integrity. "What sort of nonsense is this?" said Archie. Fed up, I replied, "The sort of nonsense that will give me a career and respect. Darling Archie, will all your…" I cleared my throat "wealth and your perfect upperclass manners, what have you produced in your life that have added some value to it?" I turned my back to him. Right then, the narcissist permanently lost his center role in my life. It started when I decided to address him as Archie, not Archibald.

Some time after, the exhibition in Paris took place successfully. Spencer and I had a double exhibition in Le Marais. Life is a box full of coincidences. "My father had a business in that same neighborhood," I told Spencer. I visited the streets for the first time. I waited until Archie would fall asleep drunk on the restroom floor - which he justified by stating it was cold and cozy - so I could meet my love under the streetlight near Place des Vosges. The colors of the window displays filled me with happiness, which was vividly present in my soul whenever I met Spencer. I saw a stunning window with Mardi Gras figurines; we kissed. Spencer checked his watch, "'Tis time to return. He may be awake," he said.

When we returned to London, Archie refrained from drinking too much, especially when he suspected I would leave to see Spencer. I thought maybe he already knew by then. Archie switched his meetings to avoid a stable schedule so I wouldn't advance notice of his absences. Harold's nanny seemed to watch me as well. I was again confined, only that time the coffin was bigger.

In the following days, I was unwell. The nanny perfected her spying skills, which made me even sicker to my stomach. I wanted to recover so I could meet Spencer and let him know the reason why I wasn't available. "Your state…is an interesting one," told me the nanny. "I feel like eating. Would you see to that, please?" I told her, putting her back in her place. I had to recover from the sickness the sooner the safer!

The smell of the chicken casserole made me queasy but I still ate it. The following day, when the nanny came to my room, I told her, "Your casserole made me worse! You should work diligently on your cooking skills. It was revolting! Please, don't come to my room today because I am feeling more indisposed than yesterday. I shall sleep," I concluded. She didn't seem to suspect my intentions. I actually had thrown the rest of the casserole away. At that point, I couldn't trust her. I put on a black dress and left.

I arrived at Spencer's. When I knocked on the door, his elderly neighbor Mrs. Campbell told me, "The gentleman upstairs was murdered. It was awful, blood on the walls. No one saw the killer. Actually, the young lady upstairs saw his trench coat with a queer patch, a coat of arms with a bird. That's it!" I walked away aimlessly. By the Rives Thames, my tears turned into suicidal droplets who desperately plunged into the water toward nothingness. I said to myself, "He knows."

Archie was disintegrating faster than I could keep up. After the exhibition in Paris, the only people allowed in my company were Harold and the nanny. The other staff members were invisible to me. The nanny took charge of everything. I started playing the role of content housewife, as my belly grew bigger and bigger. I was running out of ideas to disguise my "interesting state," as the nanny had said before.

I returned home, curled my body under the sheets, hugged the pillow, and cried. Harold and I were in danger. I kept thinking about the murder, Archie's disruptive behavior, his coldness in marrying me to keep his money. A familiar consideration came to my mind, "I need a new escape plan." I was always on the run. It was evident the nanny had noticed my absence because when Archie came back, he sparked a fight. "How are you feeling today?" he inquired, slurring his speech. As the argument increased, he grabbed my arms and shoved me down the stairs, causing a miscarriage. I bled profusely. The red stains on my clothes told me the story of an angel whose broken wings denied him the chance to be born. My baby was robbed of the pain and joy of living.

When I recovered from my condition, Archie made

himself drunker each day, and his presence more evident. I began to ask him for money to buy fancy fabrics to make dresses for our outings, to pay the designer, and a little extra for etiquette lessons with a certain Mrs. Bancroft. That was my plan to have emergency money in order to save my son's life and mine. I opened a private bank account to deposit the funds.

One day, I arrived home from the bank. I searched for Harold but he nowhere in the property. The nanny had also disappeared so I suspected she kidnapped him. Archie appeared by the library door, "We do not need a nanny for Harold. He is now at a boarding school for boys until he turns 18. Good luck seeing him now," he challenged me. "Monster! You took my son from me," I said. I hit him uncontrollably wherever I could. I continued, "No one will ever love you. You were never loved, that's why you don't know how to love. You just don't have it in you."

He slapped me so hard I fell against the banister by the base of the stairs. We both stopped eating for about a week. Firstly, because of how we both felt; Secondly, due to the fact we had no servants anymore. He then drank more and more and I fell ill due to my weakness so I phoned a doctor acquaintance who arranged me to go to a hospital, assuring me my situation would be kept private.

Little did I know Archie paid constant visits to me at the hospital and became very close to my nurse. The sun rays woke me up one morning from a one-thousand-year sleep. My drowsiness made me unable to move appropriately. I closed my eyes when the nurse came in. I saw her replacing my actual medication with different pills. She was doping me. "Wake up. Medication time," she said. I pretended to yawn, took the fake pills into my mouth but didn't swallow them. I laid down to think.

Next day, the nurse came back. I was ready for her. When

she turned her back, I hit her head. Holding my heavy breathing was the hardest thing to do, but I had to manage. I stripped her off then redressed her in my gown. I placed her carefully in the hospital bed, stole the dopey pills from her pocket, put her uniform on, and fled the scene. In the hospital hallway, I found out the room where the nurses placed their belongings. I went there, stole a dress, and a pair of shoes. "Have a lovely day," I said to the receptionist as I walked out, shaking inside.

At home, one of Archie's mistresses was on her way out the door. I watched them until I made sure she left. I found him smoking a cigar in the backyard. "Surprise," I told him. "I was waiting for my dismissal today. Isn't that lovely? Would you care for some breakfast?" I asked. He nodded in shock. I made the best breakfast I could and doped him with the pills I stole from the nurse. When he fell sound asleep in the living room chair, I rushed to the library. I opened the safe and discovered where Harold's boarding school was located. I also found out Archie had a plan to murder me and replace me with a fake wife so he wouldn't lose the inheritance. I went through his wardrobe, picked the most stuck-up men's outfit, put on enough make-up to make me look manly then went to the kitchen downstairs and cut off the black bristles from a rough brush in order to improvise a fake beard.

On my way to Harold's boarding school, my heart jumped out of my mouth. I began panting. "What am I doing?" I said to myself. The first stop was the bank to collect all the emergency money I had deposited for a safe future.

The second stop was the boarding school where I saw Harold for the last time. He was cheerful, playing with others boys. "He seems happy. I want to make sure he is kept in his studies until he attends university. Am I clear?" I told the Director. "He is in good hands here. I understand, sir," he replied.

At the school, I knew my son would be safe. I paid his tuition and boarding until he would turn 18. I was sure Archie wouldn't be able to remove him from school because I emphasized to the Director that I - Archie his father - was moving to the countryside to care for an illness and couldn't possibly be bothered to take care of Harold so, in case I changed my mind in the future, to please disregard my subsequent change of plans. After that encounter, my words assured me Archie would never be able to harm my son Harold.

I purchased a trip to New York City, still in disguise. "It's for my wife and I," I said, clearing my throat. I bought two tickets to not raise any suspicion because trust was a challenging road and I had to make sure Archie wouldn't be able to stop my plans before they came to fruition.

At home, in the living room, Archie tried to choke me. I seized hold of the table lamp and hit him in the head, causing his forehead to bleed. "I will kill you," he yelled then ran after me. I ran to the bedroom upstairs, packed my luggage with the few clothes I was able to carry without effort, and left through the second floor window.

Before leaving England to a new land, I used the men's room to change into my female attire. When I walked out, a gent starred at me shocked. There I was, free again!

CHAPTER 11

In 1951, The City of New York was a dichotomy: the commotion of life and death walking a fine line. Painting reminded of Spencer so I gave it up. I took to writing nonfiction when I moved into a tenement apartment in the Lower East Side. I still have fond memories of the children making a splash on the street below my window, playing with the water leaking from the broken sprinkler. The water seemed to wash off their troubles. Suddenly, their joy contaminated the entire street. Other children played with a ball on the corner. Whenever a boy named Billy kicked the ball, he ended up breaking the baker shop window. Billy was known for his terrible aim but the other boys thought it to be funny to see the look on the baker's eyes when he realized the shattered glass once again. The kids laughed their way through life, starring at the baker Mr. Thompson, as I recall.

In the evening, the fire escape staircase overflowed with children when it was boiling hot inside. Those little angels blessed my evenings. I would sit one floor above them and work on my nonfiction to document this new animal called New York City. It was wild, thrilling, and to me it represented a place of opportunities. New York gave me a new life with its jazz clubs, coffeehouses, music, theatre, chorus girls, fancy restaurants, speedy pedestrians, speedier cars.

An 8-ear-old girl with curly hair and thin as a toothpick, whose eyes were as sweet as honey, poked me in the arm one day. "I'm Cora. Who are you?" Cora asked me. "Hannah. You can call me, Hannah," I replied. From then on, a friendship developed between that cute little child and I. Cora would come every night and beg me to hum a tune, which ended up being a makeshift nursery rhyme whose lyrics I had forgotten. "That's sad!" she once said. "Sing me a happy song. Do this," she commanded as she snapped her fingers. Her whole being went spinning to the sound of her imaginary music. Cora's fantasy world was infectious. I then peeked beyond the fire escape structure and New York glowed. Cora noticed me looking away then said, "What's the matter?" I turned back to her and said, "The City is so magical at night." She then asked me full of curiosity, "What do you write in your book?" I replied, "I write about you, about me, New York, this street. I write about life!"

There was no room for Sadie in my life any longer. Hannah gave me freedom, peace, and love at the end of the tunnel. Once in a while, I still scanned my soul for Sadie's remains. She wasn't necessarily dead. She would lie dormant, waiting for the right moment to come out of her shell and play.

Needless to mention, the tenement where I lived was

rather rundown. The building complex was a duo of two constructions that resembled the barracks in Auschwitz. Between them, there were wires that the tenants used for clotheslines. The humidity in the clothing combined with the smell of the beggarly apartments and the awful steam that came out of the streets and buildings everywhere made me frequently unwell. Yet the possibility of renewal excited me. New York was a creature I still had to tame. Maybe it was time to summon Sadie from her slumber so she could help me come up with ideas on how to improve my appearance and land a job. After all, all the pearls that were thrown her way needed to be of service in my new existence. I was being parsimonious with my funds. On the other side of the token, I was in desperate need to leave the poverty-stricken life I was leading. I had to spend a little to gain a little in return.

I went for a stroll in the park. The balmy breeze on my face gave me thoughts of independence. I noticed a fabrics store. I used my limited funds to purchase what would be a fine elegant dress. Also needles, threads, and so on. I left the premises giggling naively like Cora.

On my way home to start working on my new outfit, I passed by a newsy boy who dropped one of his papers. The news on the front page landed flat on the ground. It said,"Wealthy British Man Dead In The Bowery." I learned that Archie came to New York looking for me, obsessed with bringing me back to London. "How much?" I asked the newsboy. I paid him and walked the streets absent-minded. When Archie arrived in New York, he spent the rest of his money paying a swindler, who passed as a legitimate private investigator, to search for me. When he went broke, he ended up in the Bowery where a fellow homeless got in an altercation with him. Archie was stabbed in his heart and left lung. He died on the spot. The murderer buried him in the snow.

His body was found stiff days later with his documents in the back pocket of his corroded slacks.

"Call Harold's school," I said to myself. I called and tried to arrange for a future meeting as soon as my finances improved. Unsuccessfully! Defeated, I continued on my walk back home, determined to make the best dress for my brand-new self. My energetic attitude produced a stunning dress. I was grasping at straws so the dress had to land me a job. I hung it by the bed, safe from the children. Since I shared a room with critters again, I had to preserve the my creation as intact as possible.

"You're trespassing, Mr. Mouse. No loitering in this property," I jokingly told the rodent in my room.

Although I felt a bit stir crazy since I arrived, I used that time to work on myself to be a better person. I say that because, nowadays in later years, I read about so many cases of those struggling with depression, anxiety, and other mental health issues merely because they were locked in. I then thought to myself, "Can't these people live with themselves? If they can't live with themselves, who would want to?" It's incomprehensible that people who feel confined would use that situation as an excuse to hurt others. I lived and survived the Holocaust, was forced to be locked in and I didn't decide to go around murdering, stabbing, and raping people. What is wrong with humanity if humans deprive themselves of what should be inherent in them? Humans should be more humane. Love thy neighbor!

Considering the above-mentioned issues, I wasn't immune to depression, anxiety, or isolation. I just chose to use them in a positive way. How could I become a better person? How could I help my neighbor more effectively? And I still saved time to appreciate beauty behind the ugly, scary birds, the malnourished children sleeping in the sad fire escape, and the sun rays, which penetrated through the interstices of the cadaverous tree branches. I saw life, where there wasn't!

That evening, I had nightmares about the dress. In my dream, it became alive and ordered me to hide in a corner, be afraid, and conform. The dress had a sickly green aura. Out of the blue, a bright white light hit from the sky and the dress was purified by it, made white with a ghostly twinkle.

The next day, I left in my new outfit. New York was a relaxing town on a Sunday morning. I ventured into one of the Rockefeller neighborhoods so I could have an idea where to look for a job. I stumbled upon a cutesy flower shop for the riches. I stepped in when I saw a sign about a job. "How can I help you?" the florist asked. "I am here for the sign. It says looking for help," I said. I was hired on the spot to design the flower shop window displays. That job gave me the peace I really longed for. "Flowers don't hurt people," I thought to myself. Besides, there was no such thing as working long, abusive hours at the flower shop. The customers could be demanding. On the other hand, I wasn't the salesperson, I didn't have to deal with that part of the business so I rested in my corner. I came in everyday to change the arrangements with freshly picked gardenias, camellias, tulips, dahlias, orchids, and roses. Plenty of beautiful roses in red, yellow, and white.

When I received my first pay, I saved a small portion of my funds to purchase a black fancy dress. I passed by the department store everyday on my way home before boarding the train. There, was the black dress! So I bought it. I couldn't quit my day job at the flower shop. But to be able to leave the tenement, I needed to find a second job at night. I hung the black dress at home. I starred at it. What was it telling me? Cora knocked on my window, she came up the staircase to see me. "You disappeared!" she said. "How could I disappear? I am here, aren't I?" I replied. We smiled. At her request, I sang a happy jazzy tune I learned on the subway station where a man played his saxophone and a lady sang. The song hammered in my head for a while so my brain gave up on forgetting it by then. Soon, I was able to reproduce it better than the singer. I developed my singing skills in New York but show business wasn't for me, I knew that. So, I sang to Cora. "This is beautiful. Can you teach me?" she begged. "Please, please," she insisted. "Yes! Now it's time for bed. Good night, Cora," I told her.

Cora left my window half-open to allow some air in and left through the stairs. She lived with 8 siblings, her mom and dad, and her grandma who seemed to come by to stay when she visited from her apartment two floors above theirs. The tenement was overcrowded. Often times, there was a fire in a building somewhere in the vicinity, from which no one escaped. The flames would mesmerize the onlookers much like the tragedy of Bread and Circus in Roman times, much like our current 2023 TV shows portraying violences as if they were the norm. Well, that's just so unfortunate!

One day, I woke up a bit late and rushed to work. In New York, I was expandable again. At least, my job was and I didn't want to be replaced. I felt so anxious I cursed the train for not moving any faster. As I got off, I ran and slipped on an ice-cream spill. "Are you ok?" someone asked me. As I got up, I replied, "Yes, thank you." She was a stunning Black lady with a tidy updo, perfect dark complexion, full lips covered in light red liptstick, and a friendly, bubbly character. "I'm Eleanor." "Hannah, very pleased." She grabbed make-up out of her purse and concealed the bruise on my right cheek. "There, now it's much better," she said. "Thank you. You are so kind. I'm sorry for being in a hurry. I really have to go. It's so difficult to find a job in New York," I told her. "Hey, why don't you come and see me at work one of these days? I sing, at a nightclub." She gave me the address of her workplace. "Come in on Thursdays. I'm not a big act yet so I can't get Fridays. Very nice meeting you…" she said as if trying to confirm my name. "Hannah," I told her.

The following Thursday evening, I went to the jazz club. Since I wasn't a minor, I was let in easily. Many of the chorus girls and aspiring singers faked their documents in order to work at the club, as I later found out. The orchestra gave me life. The music was contagious, loud. When the performer sang a ballad that sent me back to memory lane, I let out a shy tear, which I carefully dried with the tip of my index finger. "Something got in my eye," I told Eleanor, faking a smile. We were sitting at a table with two of her friends. Soon, it was time for her to go onstage. Her voice was angelical, sublime! It made me believe in goodness again. When her performance was over, she sat back at the table, had a hearty laugh, and ordered some spirit - the kind I don't recall. I was hypnotized by the all the brass, the ensemble, all those hearts beating at the same time, contrasting with the asymmetrical music. New York was life!

A clumsy waitress, who rather looked like a chorus girl in her extra short skirt and bedazzled sleeveless top, accidentally spilled whiskey over a rich customer. She was fired before me. I got up, asked the manager for a private word, insisted that I would make a great hire, and I secured myself a second job that very night.

Eleanor and I became the best of friends. One morning, she took me to Harlem. I was reticent, at first. As a predominantly Black neighborhood, I didn't want to feel like an outsider again. "During the first war, Harlem had a huge Jewish community. Didn't you know? Besides, you are with me," she said. Her words reminded me I forgot to search for my relatives since my arrival. I knew nothing about them or their whereabouts. That meant I wasn't able to reconnect with my siblings after they were sent to live here in order to escape Hitler.

"Don't cry," Eleanor said. "It's a lovely day," she added. Indeed, it was. We walked the streets of Harlem, it was Sunday. The African-American ladies wore extravagant hats, well-cut dresses, and shiny shoes. It was church mass. Eleanor and I weren't attending any religious ceremony, though. She wanted to show a different flavor of the city so I absorbed every second of it. I took her Downtown, we stopped at a delicatessen, bought two sandwiches, and went up to Central Park for a nice picnic. And the hovering doves blessed our friendship. She told me she was in love with Ray, a tall, handsome, saxophone player from the band. "I remember him. He looked at you when you sang," I shared. "He wants to marry me," she confided. Ray seemed like a nice person, for what I could tell. At that point, I was 24 years old but was able to figure anyone out with a quick glance, and he seemed like a nice fella.

At the flower shop, my shifts proved a haven in comparison to my evening job at the nightclub. In the morning, it was blissful! At night, the silly hands of the patrons, the loud Bebop insisting on blowing my ear drums, the cattiness of the chorus girls… By week's end, I was overworked, overwhelmed, under-loved. In August, 1951, I fell ill. My body had worked so hard that every single muscle complained possibly as loud as the Bebop. I was feverish, sweaty, clammy. Then I fainted to sleep!

CHAPTER 12

"There is no path to happiness. Happiness is the path." - Buddha

I turned 24 years old on August 16, 1951. After overworking for quite a while, I decided to try the train to Coney Island in order to clear my head. A day at the beach didn't sound like a bad thing to do. Besides, it was Thursday…"Wait, I'm late for work," I realized. I arrived at the flower shop only to discover I had lost my job. I walked all the way home to convince myself something good would come up, that God had a plan for me, that everything happens for a reason. Back in my room, I spent the whole day sleeping. Sometimes it is crucial to allow our minds to rest, even when others may construe our calmness as lackadaisical.

I worked that evening, and so did Eleanor. She was bubblier than ever. I didn't tell her what happened to allow her enthusiasm a chance to cheer me up. At the end of our shifts, we both sat down. That time, I was ready for a glass of Manhattan. "To my birthday!" I said. "Oh, sweety!" Eleanor said. We celebrated at the table then barhopped, chatting the night away.

I made plans to be totally free that following Sunday. Coney Island stayed in my mind. I didn't know why. I told Eleanor I wanted to rest for the day and hopped on a train to the shores of Coney. I was a mixture of curious, happy, doubtful, like the distinct ingredients of my Manhattan cocktail the previous Thursday.

I met your grandpa Avner that day, Michael. By this time, you have found my journal. I am not ashamed of my over-sharing. It compensates the years of silence about my past. We often disregard the power of therapy and I believe it would have benefitted me a while ago. However, as I bare my soul to you, my beautiful grandson, as I do my therapy in writing. I am now able to let go of the ghosts in my past. Growth is not only letting go of others' behaviors but also letting go of ours, and still be able to accept and love ourselves in the process!

The train station exploded with beachgoers. I walked around the carnival rides. The children's faces were abstract brushstrokes moving in the rides, as the sunshine caressed them. I went toward the sand, removed my shoes. To skip the rowdy families, I sat close to a man. He wore black full-rimmed square eyeglasses and read "The Stranger," by Camus. In French! "Could I sit here?" I asked him. He bobbed his head. I undressed down to my one-piece bathing suit, grabbed a towel from my bag, placed it on the sand, and sat on it. The wind blew softly on my beach hat and sent it flying. "My hat!" I said. He suddenly got up, recovered my hat and handed it to me. That time I put it in the bag. "Silly of me when it's so windy…" "Hi, I'm Avi," he introduced himself with a warm, baritone voice.

Avi told me about the book he was reading. He intro-duced me to Sartre's works and he talked about Sartre's contribution to Camus' newspaper named Combat. He told me Sartre wrote about anti-semitism against French Jews and racism against Black people. Sartre was brave enough to write against anti-semitism in post-war France. Avi also told me about other minorities and how Black people were ostracized in American culture. Minorities were excluded from the close-knit circle of middle-class and upper-class White citizens. In a witty referral to the ruling class, he said, "Citizens they are! They have access to layers of socio-economic improvements that other people are denied." I was hooked: a Jew and an intellectual!

By the end of the day, my hand caressed his timid forearm, and we kissed. I realized I had never been in love before. When I had feelings for Ethan, it was an idealized form of love. With Avi, it was the actual thing. While we kissed, all the clocks in the world seemed to stop. Time was suspended. I felt eternal, loved, embraced, all at once.

We got off in Greenwich Village where he had a studio apartment. "You can stay, if you wish," he said. "It's cold outside," I quickly replied. "It's summer!" he added, pointing at the hot weather outside the window.

I walked home to the Lower East Side, trying to avoid passing by the Bowery. Avi and I met several other times until we got to know each other better. Trust must be built! He invited me that year to watch the Macy's Thanksgiving Parade. I remember the Rockville Centre High School Marching Band, the NYPD Mounted Unit, Rudolph The Red-Nosed Reindeer, the float with Foodini, The Great, the Cinderella's Coach, and the wilting Rainbowfish, which was hooked to a lamppost around the Columbus Circle area but got punctured and drooped to the ground on 8th Avenue. Afterward, Avi had to work on his novel but he invited me to his studio to chat a bit more. It wasn't only the Rainbowfish that blew that day, so did my belly.

In 1952, I had your mother, Michael. Evie was born without any complications at a sterile hospital. Eleanor came to visit but I heard she had been barred from entering the facility because she was colored. I collected all my strength and, still in my hospital gown, rushed down the stairs to the main entrance. I managed to reach Eleanor before she left. She was crying outside on a corner. "You just come on in!" I told her. The receptionist came to prevent me from bringing her in and tried to hold me. "You lay your hands off me. I just had a baby. Shame on you all! Just think…" I pointed at my head in order to make myself understood to all the simpletons, "Just think, being White, or Black, or Jewish isn't something you choose. If you were born Black, or Jewish would you think it's right to treat other people this way? This is Eleanor and she'll come up with me to see her godchild. Now excuse ourselves," I said, leaving them motionless. Eleanor had a twinkle in her eye. We went up the stairs to the room. Reluctantly, the nurse brought Evie for us to see. "Isn't she lovely?" Eleanor said.

Years went by, Eleanor had moved to Chicago and we lost touch, unfortunately. I don't believe she made a name as a singer because she kept mentioning her wish to have a baby, marrying Ray the sax player, and moving closer to family in Chicago. Evie wasn't baptized by Eleanor. It was just my white lie to right an injustice.

The day Evie was born, Avi asked me not to return to the nightclub gig. He told me to take my writing seriously because he believed something great would come out of it someday. And I quit! His sensitive, respectful personality didn't push me to be what I wasn't, didn't try to crush me for who I was. He was the lead character in his life with his own priorities and likes, and I was the lead character in mine. People who are truly in love, we respect each other. If you love someone, Michael, you love them the way they are, you don't try to change them, or their tastes, or their priorities. But I am not here to patronize you, forgive me, my handsome reader.

In 1962, Evie turned 10 years old. I was 35 then; Avi, 36. Before summer died down, your grandpa and I took your mom to Central Park. Evie loved the gondola ride every time the vessel pat the water, making it blush with ripples. She enjoyed when the three of us hopped on a horse carriage ride. "No, I want the white horse, daddy," she commanded. "Next time, dear," I replied. Avi heeded to her demands and she became increasingly difficult.

Before the High Holy Days, we took Evie to the F.A.O. Schwartz so we could have ideas of toys she may want. Avi and I were not set in stone about any religion so we preferred to look at it from a nondenominational approach. Thus, whatever the toy Evie chose, it didn't matter. She decided she wanted a doll. It was the ugliest thing I had ever seen! Maybe because it reminded me of dead children in Auschwitz. The doll was motionless just like the infants' corpses. I did not say a word to your grandfather about her keeping the doll. I kept my resilient self in check.

Our days went by in a perfect combination of silence, meals, and school schedules. When I dropped Evie off at school, I prepared breakfast for Avi and then we went to our separate desks to work on our writing, not always in the same order. Our home was a creative haven and it was customary to hold dinners for poets, writers, musicians, dancers, singers, philosophers, university professors. We had a wooden plaque made just to hang on our front door. It said,"Open minds and open hearts."

Avi was working hard on his third novel. To the same extent, I was immersed in my article on anti-semitism and Sartre. That's when Evie became intolerable. The constant interruptions...! She didn't seem to understand that her parents spent quality time with her but when we were at work she needed to respect it. One of Avi's cousins came to take care of Evie. However, when we both delved deeply into our work, Evie turned indifferent. I had complaints from school like, "Your daughter, Ma'am, pushed little Tony off the swing, and she stayed there just watching." Another one said, "Evie carefully lifted a girl's hair, put the gum in it, and pushed hard down the girl's long hair. She had to cut it off!" the Principal told me.

The sole music that would calm my ears then was listening to Chet Baker's Cool Jazz. It soothed me well. Avi soon became a fan. Mr. Baker's voice reminded me that life was uncomplicated, that the joy of being alive, the contentment, the gratitude was all there. It only relied on each person to acknowledge life's simplicity, and to be grateful for the gift.

Avi and I took your mom to the 1962 Macy's Thanksgiving Parade. It was Evie's first time. I don't recall anything about the parade that year. My head revolved around my work and how to improve the world yet my world with Evie was lacking any betterment. I guess we can only do the best we can and hope for a positive outcome. My mind was choppy during the parade, for I wasn't concentrated in work. My job was true bliss!

After the parade, we stopped by a coffeehouse. Evie ordered "hot chocolate with a marshmallow on top!" she said. "Here, a napkin. Can you write marshmallow?" Avi asked her. Evie wrote "marshemellow." We laughed. "What's so funny?" Evie inquired. Avi changed the conversation, "Do you know the origins of Thanksgiving?" he asked her. She looked confused. I hid my quirky smile. Avi added, "In the 1600s, in England, a group of people the Protestants were persecuted just because of the way they practiced their faith. Around 1620, the Pilgrims decided to escape on a ship called

The Mayflower. Evie's eyes grew in awe, "Ahhh!" Avi resumed, "People were mean to the Pilgrims in England so they ran away on a boat to another land. They arrived here in Plymouth Rock, Massachussets. But when they arrived, they realized the food they knew wasn't available, there were no homes like theirs, and the cold, harsh winter made their life very difficult. At the time, The Wampanoags, a tribe of Native Americans, helped them find resources to build a home, taught them how to grow different foods, and some of the Pilgrims survived the winter, the hunger, and being without a home. Just you imagine, Evie."

She starred at him, not missing a beat of the story. Then she asked, "What is a protestor?" We laughed again. Avi continued, "Protestant! Back to our story, a year passed by and the surviving Pilgrims invited the most important leaders of the Wampanoags to have a harvest dinner with them, as a sign of gratitude." "Tell me more," Evie requested. Avi resumed, "Two centuries later, in 1863, there was this very important lady named Sarah Josepha Hale. Our country was divided in half, it was the Civil War. The southerners believed in enslaving people but the northerners believed that people should all be free. So, Sarah wrote to President Abraham Lincoln to request that Thanksgiving be made into a National Holiday because she wanted everyone in the country to be one, to be friends with each other. President Lincoln accepted and Thanksgiving became a National Holiday! But it took two centuries." I suggested, "Oh, Avi, she's too young to understand." Evie replied, "No, I'm not. Daddy said that immigrants came from another land because people were mean to them and they had to survive making friends in a new place." Avi smiled and added, "You see? She's like us." Evie insisted, "Tell me more." Avi told her, "Fo you to understand in a few words, Thanksgiving is a story of people who were persecuted for their faith, just like us Jews. Also, a story of immigrants because those Pilgrims were not Natives. It's also a story of community. Imagine going to a place where there are no houses, no food, it's really freezing, and you don't speak the foreign language!" His story saddened her but she asked again, "Tell me more." He continued, "That's all about Thanksgiving, no more. But…nowadays the sons and daughters of the persecuted Pilgrims think it's okay to persecute other minorities. But they were minorities once, weren't they?" Evie replied, "Yes, they were. That's not right."

After a pause, I suggested, "I think we're good with storytelling today, huh?" Avi finalized, "But you know what's most interesting? Mrs. Sarah Josepha Hale who made Thanksgiving our National Holiday, she also wrote "Mary Had A Little Lamb." You remember that rhyme?" Evie went all the way back to the Village singing *"Mary Had A Little Lamb."* And Michael, forgive me for sounding sacrilegious to your Christian wife but… at the end of the trip, I still don't know if I wanted to choke Mary or the lamb.

CHAPTER 13

"Yesterday is history, tomorrow is a mystery, today is a gift of God, which is why we call it present." - Bill Keane

Evie ran away from home, leaving a note on the fridge. She was 15 years old. I went to her school to talk to one of her friends who told me she thought Evie had told me that she was leaving for San Francisco to attend a festival. "What's in San Francisco? She's 15," I said. The girl told me that Evie left like other people did to go to *The Summer of Love.* "What about you? Are you going there? Can you take me?" I asked anxiously. "My parents...I couldn't just go..." she replied.

I inquired around Evie's circle of friends unsuccessfully. I then decided to ask the principal himself. "Excuse me, thank you for having me first of all. It's a very important matter. My daughter Evie..." I wasn't able to finish the sentence. "Sit down, Ma'am. Would you like a glass of water?" he asked politely. "Thank you." My visit to his office was disappointing because no one seemed to know of her whereabouts.

It was June, 1967, when I walked home crying more than I ever did before. Work had weakened for me. Besides, I was in much need of a break. When I closed the apartment door behind me, Avi said, "Surprise! I was hired to write a movie script! They picked up one of my novels!" He was so flamboyantly happy I just didn't have it in me to piss on his dreams. I wasn't in the same emotional wavelength, although I played the part because I was truly happy for him, for us as a family. But the family was missing a member and I was incapable of breaking the news to him. I cheered and toasted to his success then we shared a couple of Martinis. When he kissed my cheek, my face dropped. "What's the matter?" he asked. I burst in tears, "Evie left." Avi asked confused, "Left? Where?" "She left…" I threw a plate across the room, "She left to San Francisco," I finally told him with the best of my anger. "Sit down, we'll figure it out," he advised me.

We conducted an investigation. We handed fliers and asked random people at the nearby park, her usual hangouts, the grocer, the baker, the police officer who patrolled outside our building in the Upper West Side where we lived then. "Ma'am, thousands of kids are headed that way. I'm sorry to say that, but all you can do is pray," advised the officer.

We strolled through Central Park, trying to make sense of Evie's decision. Since when Avi told her the origin of Thanksgiving, she stopped behaving badly at school and became a more docile child, accepting, and smart like us. "What drove her to…?" I let it out. "I have a plan. It may not be well-sketched yet but…" Avi said.

We decided to make all the arrangements to move to Los Angeles so he could start working on the movie script and I could be closer to San Francisco. "But it's a long drive," I told him. "It's the same state. That's the option we have," he answered. We paid a visit to our neighbor and best friend Amélie, a French woman our age who read all morning while smoking two packs of unfiltered Lucky Strikes then played Erik Satie's "Gnossiennes" all afternoon. "*Ça n'est pas possible! Evie est une* child!" she said. We asked Amélie to keep a close eye on the apartment, in case Evie came back. We left her the keys as well.

The plane soared as my thought drifted away in the horizon. The clouds below looked like a cotton rug, which gave me hope that God was on my side and Evie, a step away. "What's the distance from LA to San Francisco?" I said before I caught myself. Avi was sound asleep.

We arrived in the West Coast. Los Angeles didn't seem like a dream place then, at least not to me. What bothered me was the stucco on the buildings. We moved into a one bedroom on Gower wide enough to put a table for Avi to work, too small for me to breathe. "I'm leaving for San Francisco, love," I announced. "We just arrived," he replied. "I have to find my daughter!" At the end of the conversation, he was of the same mind.

I bought a 1960 Austin Healey and drove upstate. I dressed conservatively not to attract the wrong male attention on the road. Midway, I needed to stop and take a nap. I drove behind a tree in the woods to hide my vehicle. It wasn't safe for a female alone on the road "without a husband." That's the uptightness of the 60s until, by the end of the decade, the tightness became loose.

I woke up before sunset then resumed my driving upward. I rented a room at an apartment in the Pacific Heights. The fliers all over town advertised The Summer of Love, the year 1967, and the location. I walked for a long time until I ended up in Haight-Ashbury around the Panhandle. Thousands of flower children in stentorian fashions paraded around on drugs. San Francisco was a different kind of loud than New York was to me because the music was all about peace, something I was seeking for quite a while; and love, someone I was searching for at the time.

I phoned Avi to let him know I arrived well. The music seemed to flow in the air like the hair of those people, of those lost children like mine. I was overwhelmed seeing so many youngsters all over, the weather wasn't my favorite though. I bumped into the Haigh-Ashbury Free Clinics, an organization founded to provide assistance to the youth in matters of heavy drug addiction, mental health, and so on. "Maybe Evie is struggling with something," I thought. They were the kindest people and their work moved me to tears. I spent the entire months of June and August between phoning Avi to let him know I hadn't found her yet and dropping a line to Amélie in New York to find out whether or not Evie had showed up there.

At the end of August, I called Avi for the last time and he suggested we both go to New York to spend some time there to wait for Evie. The screenplay was ready and locked so he wasn't needed until further notice. There we went, back to the Big Rotten Apple!

By February 1968, Evie stormed in. "My baby!" I said in shock. Evie was very sick, and pregnant! Eight months pregnant! There weren't cell phones then so I wasn't able to tell Avi. He had left to get groceries for a dinner we scheduled with our Chavurah friends.

"Mom, I'm afraid," she said, crying. "It's going to be all right, sweetie," I said, lying to her for the first time. I rushed to Amélie and we both managed to get Evie to the hospital as soon as we could. We left to the hospital without closing the front door behind us. Avi must have been alarmed when he arrived home. When Avi finally reached us there, Evie had left us forever.

Right there, I became a Rothko painting, so blurred that

only my emotions were imprinted in my present. There was no line defining the streets, sights, and sounds of my existence. Maybe a lingering smell evoked by a red and blue masterwork of Abstract Art! I was disappearing...

Meanwhile, you - my blessed gift from God - were born. In life, one can't have everything. We must resiliently accept our victories as well as our losses.

When you turned a year old, Avi and I took you to an event. The babysitter had canceled and we either took you with us or we canceled. A lady in a red velvety dress, pretentiously said to me something cruel about bringing a child to a fancy place. She wore a diamond necklace that could probably buy a whole building. I looked at her coldly and said, "How useless it is to add price to your stones when you heart has no value." Sometimes, people can be judgmental, Michael. What did she know about my life up to that moment? Nothing!

At the end of that year, we decided to move closer to work so we packed it all to Los Angeles. Amélie and I remained close friends until her late years. Longevity is a blessing and a curse, you see. We have the impression of losing people along the way yet they still live in our memories, hidden undercover like Sadie. The blessing comes when we realize the magnitude of this whole experience called life. Isn't she gorgeous?

We landed first in San Francisco so we could say goodbye to your mom. We went to a park, my finger drew a rectangular shape and I wrote "Evie" in the center. I placed a rock on the pseudo-grave. Avi said a prayer to lay Evie's soul to rest. We spent a month in San Francisco to understand her motives. I looked at the sign "Haight-Ashbury." It made sense to me only in reverse, "Bury Ash Hate!"

The weather transmuted. The sun rays hit your curls, Michael, making you appear otherworldly. A beam of sunshine struck the dust particles in the air and the old wide trees seemed to tell so many stories about so many folks from all eras. When I met San Francisco that second time, I was free to fall deeply in love with the city, its colors, its vibrant characters, its lost children, the clouds, and the cold summers. I thought to myself, "I envy the trees, they will always stay."

I have always been this way: a person without roots; feeling the wind, light or strong, push me far away wherever I may end up. It seemed to me Evie was shaped by the same mold. Before she was rushed to the hospital, she gave me a little diary. She had documented her brief time in San Francisco. Both Sadie and Hannah needed courage to open it.

The three of us hit the road from San Francisco down to Los Angeles on a 1966 Corvair. Big Sur was, and still is, mostly deserted. Its live oaks, redwood trees, cottonwood, maples, and willows seemed to move above us. I always thought trees were static, but that time they raced voraciously above us like my thoughts of Evie. My life lightsped in wild green brushstrokes. When I looked back down at the road, I saw a black-tailed deer about to cross it. "Watch out!" I told Avi. The car skidded to a stop. Thankfully, we were all fine. The 60s were an era when people didn't advocate for seat belts so I'm glad you were ok, Michael.

I took all the strength I still had in me and opened her diary. The book told me that she fell in love with a much older guy in his mid 20s, bearded, bespectacled, scrawny, who advocated for peace but who beat her up one day until her right eye swelled three times bigger. Those who preach peace, don't have peace. The same way as those who preach God, do not have God. It seemed to me that people waste their whole lives playing games with others to gain superiority over them. They bust their ego while hurting others' feelings. It also seemed to me that most people, Michael, are so eager to convince others of whatever it is they are advocating for, be it peace, love, or God. Meanwhile they lack the very thing they preach. If you really want to improve the world then don't preach, just do it. Live your truth and message every single blessed day of your life and, by the end of the day, you'll realize someone out there is happier because of you. No one needs to know it, it's a magical secret between you and the person you helped.

Years later, around 1972, we drove up to Santa Barbara. Joni Mitchell's "Little Green" was playing on the radio, and I cried. Her voice teleported me to the time when I still had my Evie at home back in New York, a time when she was merely my 14-year-old daughter before she ran away from us. Ms. Mitchell's unblemished resonance was disarming. It felt like her voice and my soul were the same; no barriers between us. Such is the power of music! Then I thought that maybe music could make me understand Evie better as well. When we arrived in Los Angeles, I bought Joni Mitchell's cathartical album "Blue," sat on the corner, and wept. Then I fantasized about cuddling with you and your mom, on a bench, in some unknown rose garden, with wasabi green vines above us.

See you in the next chapter…

 You know you're in love when you can't fall asleep because reality is finally better than your dreams." - Dr. Seuss

We bought our home in Hancock Park in 1972, the home you inherited now that has been the one you will always remember as our family nest. You were about to turn 4 years old when I felt stuck with my self-imposed isolation and suggested to Avi, "This house is so huge. We need people. Why don't we join a synagogue, make some friends in the neighborhood. Friends, not co-workers!" He smiled then I returned the favor. I would turn 45 that year and living in the past just did not make any sense to me.

We hired a few people to manage the house. Avi suggested not to hire a nanny because it was a sensitive issue to me, not that I would have wanted to anyway. Michael, you and I spent the best years watching the birds say hello in the garden. I remember the day when you ran so fast, we were playing hide and seek, and you bumped against the ruins of an old well I hadn't even notice existed. So we would pretend you mother hid there to protect us. Whenever we took our breakfast outside I'd say, "Now…Run to the well." We would run as fast as we could toward the well and whisper, "Evie, are you there?" Then we laughed. The trapped breeze inside the well supported my white lie. I looked at your chubby cute little face. I saw how it made you happy to believe your mother was in there looking out for you. I shared the same warm feeling, though I knew about the veracity of my words.

Months went by, I joined the choir at a local synagogue for the High Holy Days season. Since I have always been accepting of everyone's beliefs, I also joined a Catholic choir. The former was really close to home and they were a progressive synagogue, right up my alley. The latter was in the Downtown area and very strict but I went for the music. After all, singing in Latin and English sounded like a good idea as well. However, I was selected to sing in Spanish, a language I didn't know then. "But I speak English, shouldn't I be placed with the English singing choir?" I asked the Musical Director then he replied, "No. You have an accent when you speak." That's the first prejudice I would experience in that choir but I stayed for the music. You see, Michael, music elevates our souls. It will always be an integral part of my life. I hope there will be plenty of it in the afterworld. When Nathan introduced me to the beauty that is Music, I intend to sing forever.

Rehearsals occurred on Monday evenings at the synagogue. I took you under my arms everywhere. People kept saying I was the cutest, youngest, most jovial mother around. At least, I can say I was your only mom so my mission was not to make the same mistakes by making sure I was there for you, not to smother but to just be. At the end of rehearsals, you were sound asleep.

After the judgement from the Musical Director during my audition with the Catholic choir, I chose not to bring you along to that one. One day, though, Avi asked me to take you with me. Rehearsals were Tuesday evenings. I showed up with you and a huge bag of Hallelujahs and Ave Marias sheet music. I was met with disapproving eyes. When you were asleep with your head resting on my big brown velvet bag, a lady said to me, "Does his mother work? Why bring a child to rehearsal?" I replied, "I am so sorry he makes so much noise," and looked at her in the eye because you, Michael, hadn't uttered a sound the whole time. People are like that. Let them do what they will, because they will! I never took you back there again.

At the synagogue, I felt at ease. The temple's Rabbi was a loving gentle man, and a gentleman. His wife matched his elegance. I was unafraid of being there, it was like an extended family where we would gather to elevate our voices to God. One evening, Avi and you watched me perform Jerusalem of Gold. I was in heaven to see the glow in your eyes after my performance when you said, "Glamma, you sing." I smiled. When you were older, you nicknamed me "Glamma," as in "Glamorous Grandma." You were so adorable, Michael.

I also enjoyed the other choir repertoire, despite the pressure of dogmatism. I wouldn't pretend to be Catholic or to conform to anything that didn't ring true to me. One day, a member of the choir kindly suggested, "You need to have more Jesus." That was the biggest insult at that place! I kindly replied, "You mean Joshua? Because Jesus was Joshua. He wasn't Catholic, he was Jewish." She turned her back in anger. Inside me, I forgave her. You see, often times people want to preach what they don't have in themselves. To me, Jesus was a man who was generous, that is, equalitarian. He was more of a hippie much like the flower children in San Francisco, like your mom, walking around in sandals not preaching but talking about peace and love. What did he get in return? War…and hate. It seems that many other influential people such as the likes of Ghandi and the great MLK also attempted to make the world peaceful. They were assassinated! I will never cease to try to find the reasons why people hurt other people. As an elderly lady in my 90s, I just cannot understand going to such measures. I experienced murder, rape, sexual assault, insane Nazi experiments, abortion, robbery, arson, kidnapped, child endangerment and negligence, terrorism by the hands of the Nazis, assault and battery, and domestic violence. I survived the Holocaust and if I were to feel entitled for my sufferings to justify that I should commit the same actions they subjected me to then… what would I become? Them? My point is: nothing justifies practicing hate, rape, murder, prejudice.

Conversely, I also learned and practiced forgiveness 0f myself and others; romantic, family, and self love; acceptance of myself, the circumstances, and reality, the things I couldn't change; faith in myself, in others, in this cold world, and in God; overcame and conquered my fears; found the courage to go on; built trust in myself, others, and the unknown; practiced selflessness with sacrifice and altruism; learned responsibility from my father and older brother and what it means to stand up for a cause in the face of adversity; and I am working on my redemption through these pages by dealing with accepting blame, remorse, and finding my salvation. I chose to focus my life on the positive instead. Choice is a power that most people neglect. I am rambling now that I am ancient. So, please don't let it distract your mind from the journal. Let's skip this chapter a few years, shall we?

Avi came in one afternoon with auspicious news. His first book was to become a Broadway musical. He asked me, "You are a writer and you have a musical background. How do you feel about cowriting it?" I was flabbergasted but said, "You know how I feel about Michael. If I dedicated myself to working long hours like you do…I don't want to make the same mistake, as I did with Evie." He added, "You must forgive yourself. You can't carry that heavy burden on your shoulders your whole life. I also worked hard when she was alive and she was more mellow with me…" Before I opened my mouth, he added, "Because girls tend to fight with their mothers, it's just natural. You never did anything wrong, sweetheart. You were the best mom ever." He gently held me by the arms so as to make me absorb what he was about to say, "And she knew it." We hugged. He pat my hair softly, which made me feel like a child again in a perfect fairytale of long warm embraces. Still, he agreed with me that I should stay with Michael only because I wasn't ready yet to delve into work.

When I sang Hatikva at the synagogue choir, Michael's eyes widened with awe. He used to sleep on rehearsals but not during the actual performances. When I came out from backstage, he ran to me, "Glamma, why you don't work?" His words hit me so hard they prompted me to ask myself where my life was going. I wasn't writing, painting, or who knows singing for a living? Avi noticed my long pause then added, "Glamma sings. Her job for now is singing, you see?" Michael smiled again.

That week, I secured myself a job with a political magazine that also focused on democracy, socio-economic issues, and so on. While you played around my desk, Michael, I worked on my article titled "The Color Purple and Democracy." In previous times, only the elites wore the color purple. It represented royalty, elegance, and wealth. For a long time in history, purple dye was obtained by killing thousands of sea snails named "murex" in the sea of Tyre, Lebanon. The so-called Tyrian purple required intense labor as well, causing it to be highly valued and, consequently, a tool for snobbery.

Along the centuries, other resources democratized the specific pigment so that the masses could also be seen proudly displaying their purple garb. When the magazine the article, it was well-received and it became a source of pride to me for being able to learn so much about the relationship between Democracy and, who knew, the color purple.

In 1978, I had a surprise party. As I recall, I had forgotten about my birthday. You were excellent at keeping the secret from me, Michael. You were only 10. When I turned the key, I also turned the lights on then I instantly turned 51. Turn, turn, turn! "Surprise," said the guests. By then, I knew I would be your "Glamma." The 70s were a flowy time of Halston dresses, Furstenberg wrap-arounds, disco, blue metallic eye shadow, glistening golden bodies constantly refilled with the next drug. The flower children of the 60s met their deaths in the overindulgence of the 70s to the beat of Rock'n'Roll.

Despite all the turmoil on the streets, those were happy years for me. As usual, Avi worked from home on his screenplays, musicals, novels, and had a teaching position at a Parisian university. I spent half of my time between you and my writing assignments. Late afternoons proved to be the best time to sit outside in the garden and have a hearty picnic.

I cannot claim myself as witness to the freedom the LGBT community in 70s New York because I had decided not to revisit the city ever again because it would poke my memories and not in the best of ways. But I can speak sincerely about San Francisco. There, freedom was in the air. People were fed up with the Government and Watergate, much like the 60s flower children were fed up with the Vietnam War. Freedom seemed cool enough for a change.

You were only 10 when I took you to San Francisco in September. I wanted to clear my mind before taking on another writing gig. I came up with an excuse to the Principal so that you could miss class for 3 days. We just had to add Saturday and Sunday to make it a 5 day trip. I enjoyed sitting by the hotel window and read to you, anything by Dr. Seuss. Your favorite was "The Cat in the Hat." "Glamma, can you read 'The Wizard of Oz?' Remember we watched the movie?" you asked me. When I ran out of options, we saw a copy of "The Giving Tree," forgotten in a drawer. At the end of the book, though I know how much it is beloved by so many, I was enraged. I challenged your mind with my interpretation of the book. My analysis of the book spit out, "I don't understand that kid. He asks the tree for everything but gives nothing in return until the tree, his best friend, dies. This is selfish! I will not read that again!"

I felt horrible in the following days after my outburst of anger toward the book because it reminded me of the day when your grandpa told your mom about the origins of Thanksgiving. After that encounter with reality, Evie was never the same. She and you needed to be a bit older to hear a full account of what reality is, politically and socio-economically. A child is not ready to hear the full story. On my analysis behalf though, I stand my ground to say that the book seemed as inappropriate for a child as were our observations. As a person who praises individuality, I should have kept those remarks to myself so as to not influence you, even if I was sure how mature you were then.

On the last day of our trip, we went to a record store in Haight-Ashbury. We bought a few albums, put them in the bag, stopped for sandwiches, and meandered until we ended up in Dolores Park. You were tired but that meant you were going to sleep all the way back to LA so I was happy. "Glamma, why is that man naked?" you asked me. "Look up, a cool red airplane," I quickly replied, diverting your attention from the man in leather-clad undies.

All the freedom of the 70s would have consequences in the 80s. Why does anyone have to pay a price just by being their true selves? Why does peace, love, and freedom cost more than a present day one-hundred-million dollar estate up on Mulholland Drive?

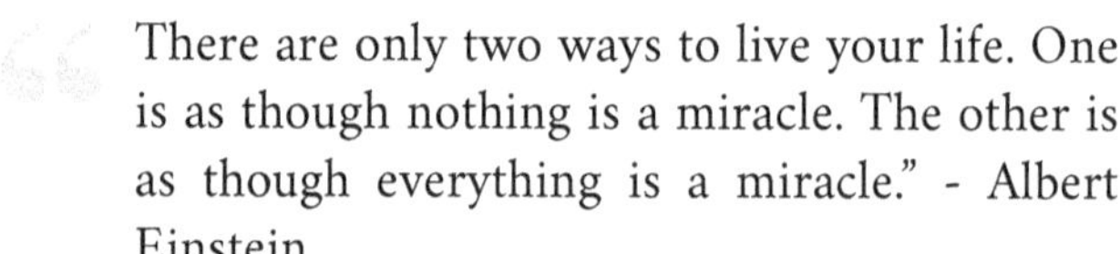

CHAPTER 15

There are only two ways to live your life. One is as though nothing is a miracle. The other is as though everything is a miracle." - Albert Einstein

The AIDS epidemic swept most of my gay friends. The 80s saw me less religious and more all-inclusive than ever. In 1981, after your Bar Mitzvah, I started my activism. I couldn't just see people dying around me while I stared from afar. I thought of the time when you asked me why I didn't have a job after I sang "Hatikvah." Your wise question had infused me with hope then. I arranged for a tutor so your days were filled with school and tutoring time. Avi was in hiatus because of an issue between the producer and the director so he went to Lake Tahoe to relax from the stressful quarrels on set.

I joined the short-lived Center for Forgiveness and Gratitude. We catered to everyone suffering post-diagnosis discrimination by providing counseling and a place to sleep, when the budget allowed us. The work exhausted me emotionally and psychologically. I was horrified when I witnessed numberless deaths that happened at the bat of an eyelash. A couple of months into it, Avi came back down from Lake Tahoe to join me at work. "What am I doing not helping you? You are my light," told me Avi.

We watched a VHS tape of a theatre production of "South Pacific." The song "You've Got To Be Carefully Taught" came on the screen. My little busy head couldn't help but draw a parallel between Reagan's anti-gay policies and the song's message. Despite the tape's constant distortions, the image was clear like water throughout the song. I thought about its message that hate is taught to children as early as possible by placing a veil before them so that they won't accept whoever may be physically or culturally different from them, the idea of internalized hate, and the fact that the character had to live in an island. Then it came to me that island was for isolation what racial hatred was for early teaching. In the same train of thought, the three words the Nazis used to have control over people *Kinder, Küche, Kirche* that is Children, Kitchen, Church. The Ku Klux Klan and their extermination of Black people in the South are related to the sentiment infused into the Third Reich's three Ks. The Nazis controlled what their *Kinder* were "carefully taught" by their mothers who represented the Kitchen under the umbrella of a fake *Kirche*, that is the church. Who murders and hates more than pseudo-religious people? Those who claim Jesus as their own while condemning others under the pretense of purity are full of filth in their soul. Then I thought of Reagan's "let them die" attitude toward gays, which very much resembles the extermination of Jews in the camps during WWII. The extermination of Jews, Blacks, gays, the Roma, and others bear a strange similarity: to kill what's different! Why? Because children need to be carefully taught to hate, people are not born hating others, that's the point. The people who upset those pseudo-religious people most are the Roma because they dare to live free outside of society's leash, not rules. That's the beauty of "South Pacific!"

In 1985, after extensive forensic testing, the remains of the Angel of Death Josef Mengele were confirmed beyond scientific doubt. To illustrate the paragraph above, the cruelest Nazi SS physician ever Mengele was living in Brazil where he found refuge. Brazil has a long history of military coupe and torture. In the 30s, the then-President Getulio Vargas paraded with Nazi-affiliated officials, and structured his government in identical fashion. The Brazilian military was trained by the Gestapo. There were concentration camps in the states of Rio de Janeiro and Sao Paulo, for instance, to host Italians and Germans - suspected of being Jews! If the suspicion turned out to be a fact, they were deported to their deaths. Unfortunately, many German-Jews went sent back to the Führer straight from Brazil. Eventually, Vargas committed suicide. Just like Hitler!

At the Center one morning, the receptionist called me to see a newcomer. "He's a patient," she told me indicating he needed professional medical care. "He had no place to go so I didn't know what to do. Can you please see him?" she added. I rushed to the front door to find a man probably in his 20s but looking about 60. His boney structure was sucked in like those in Auschwitz. With sarcomas all over his face, he pleaded, "I need your help." "Call Dr. Schwartz," I suggested to the receptionist. Dr. Schwartz was a good friend of mine. He once mentioned that in case of emergencies, he'd recommend the best hospital, which in plain English meant the patient would receive care right away. It worked like a type of medical voucher in very rare cases. We took the man to a room in the back and I had a déja-vu, "Just like Nathan!" We improvised a bed and the girl left the room to make the call. The man trembled seismically, holding my hands then he asked, "Please, stay with me. It's getting dark." He died before the receptionist even touched the phone. Sobbing, I told him, "Fly away, butterfly!" and I closed his eyes to hide myself in the janitor's room and cry.

In 1986, the Center was forced to close. I retired from everything. Looking back, it was careless of me to step out of the picture when I was still needed. But we are humans, after all, and I convinced myself it was a wise decision to retire after fighting and winning numberless wars. I had no more energy to give, maybe not even to you because I was then 59 and you, 18. Although I don't know it as a fact - you never voiced it to me - but I believe that my 59-year-old self reminded you of death. And Death reminded you of your mom. But if that isn't the truth and I am overthinking it, what teenager wants to spend time with their older relatives anyway? I understand, Michael.

One night, you came in with your high school sweetheart Kelly, a British-American daughter of two British diplomats. Avi and I gave our blessing to both of you. The love in your eyes was obvious. It was whimsical to see you experience love, as I myself was young and naïve once. Young love has an aura of purity, even if the intentions aren't always as pure. But you were two white doves in love. "I liked her from the start," I told you in the kitchen when you asked about my unbiased approval. Her folks were great people as well. I was so happy for you and still am.

Around 1991, the newfound HIV meds improved drastically to allow room for survival. Hatikvah gained a new meaning when I recovered the hope that those suffering from the epidemic would be able to see another sunrise. I turned 64 but you weren't there. No, it's not a Jewish grandmother's blame game, you simply were not able to come. I understand. Avi and I flew to London to attend your wedding that year. Kelly was stunning in her pearl-adorned organza dress, and you were so gallantly handsome.

On the plane back to Los Angeles, Avi gave the first signs of dementia.

> Yesterday is gone. Tomorrow has not yet come. We have only today. Let us begin." - Mother Theresa

Yesterday, 72 years ago, my hero Lubavitcher Rebbe accepted the mantle of leadership. Yesterday, 72 years ago, Evie was a seed. Yesterday, 72 years ago, Sadic became Hannah.

Watching the news nowadays I realize how serious society's fixation with death is. Crime series, murder, rape, horror movies. I once asked a friend the reason why she only watched crime and murder, to which she replied, "It reminds me that my life isn't that bad." That statement made me feel sorry for that person because her juxtaposition was so weak as to compare her own existence to Death. Then I asked myself why would anyone spend their life feeding their brain with pain? Why would I choose to celebrate death when I only have life in me? I was suddenly filled with peaceful bliss. I realized how lucky I was to be able to see beyond appearances and face reality without the veil of ignorance. Now, ignorance due to lack of knowledge is justifiable because one doesn't know any better. Contrastingly, ignorance as a choice because one refuses to accept the facts, reality, the truth, that in itself is a sign of Evil. Unfortunately, in 2023, I realized that there's a lot of the latter going on as we see mobs storming into democratic buildings, bringing murder and mayhem to feed the blood-thirsty neo-Nazi need for power. It's a shame that facts don't seem to matter anymore. Even the Germans deny their knowledge of the Holocaust!?! That baffles me because I am a living proof it happened. Unfortunately, my friends and relatives are not. They died, I survived. I am a fox, after all.

Avi passed away ten years ago in 2003, and I was again left alone. Alone, but not lonely. I resumed my painting, even it reminds me of someone dear, my poor Spencer, but I don't see it as cheating because Avi was the real love of my life.

It's 2023, I don't move around the house as much. I pay Xochitl very well to only sit here and help me out doing insignificant chores, just to pretend I am busy. The cleaning crew comes once a week. I don't even go upstairs but I asked Xochitl to put this journal up there for you to find, Michael. She is a great 25-year-old Mexican-American girl who dreams of becoming a scientist. I support her dreams with a tuition bonus. Imagine the doors of opportunity unlocking to her who once owned this land? She told me her name means "beautiful flower." Then I though of Evie, the 60s, the flower children, you and I in the garden talking to the well.

To celebrate Xochitl's name, I asked her to play one of my records. She turn the turntable on and raised the volume, as per my instructions. Many young people are unfamiliar with older technology. She placed the arm on the record, the needle made a full sound like a beating heart. Vinyl is still groovy! We listened all afternoon to one single song Cass Elliot's "Make Your Own Kind Of Music." Do your thing,

Michael. Never mind what others try to label you, you just go straight ahead fiercely. Be your best self, my grandson and son! Yes, I claim you as my son too! I dedicate this journal to you. This world is cold but we can both warm it up a little bit, can't we? Always maintain your integrity no matter what you face in life and the universe will shower you with blessings.

Xochitl is heading out for her classes, I'll go say goodbye to her.

(Pause)

Every inch of my body hurts at this age. I want you to open the last page. Close to the lower left corner, there's a hollow area. The Blue Sapphire earrings are there, I want you to give them to your daughter on my behalf. Like my father used to say, "they will protect your spirit." It'll give her mental, physical, emotional, and spiritual health. Hold the earrings in your hands, as I share my last words with you.

I remember one winter when we watched the movie version of "Carousel" by Rodgers and Hammerstein. As artists, they brought us "You've Got To Be Carefully Taught," giving everyone a hint to see through the veil of racism, even those who were carefully taught early in life. They also brought us "You'll Never Walk Alone" from Carousel, and souls in distress were never hopeless again. That winter night, we watched it, and I shed a timid teardrop. You asked me then, "Glamma, why are you sad?"

A last toast to you, Michael, "L'haim! To health!" I guess if this journal were one of Avi's scripts, this would be the part where I died.

"Next year..."

ACKNOWLEDGMENTS

Thank you, Ana, for being the inspiration for my lead character Hannah. You are a bright light in this world!

A huge thank you note to Vladimir de Seville who taught me to not hate back, even in the face of brutal violence.

ABOUT THE AUTHOR

Erik Whitman is an emerging fiction writer. This is his autobiographic debut novel.